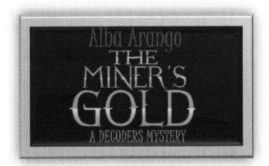

Published by Sapphire Books
P.O. Box 753842
Las Vegas, NV 89131

Book Cover and Illustrations by Jeanine Henning.

Printed in the United States of America.

For information regarding permission, write to Sapphire Books
P.O. Box 753842. Las Vegas, NV 89136

Library of Congress Control Number: 2019900828

ISBN: 978-1-7327321-5-5 (Paperback)

To Mamy and Papy

Thank you for always believing in me.

CONTENTS

1 THE MINER FORTY-NINER

Steve felt his heart quicken in excitement as he stared at the cell phone lying at the center of the coffee table in his living room. "Are you serious?"

Jack Evan's laughter came through the speakerphone. "I am. The movie set I'm working on is near the old mining town of Shakesville, where, rumor has it, there's a secret mound of buried gold left behind by a forty-niner back in the day." Jack had worked on the movie set of the Decoders second mystery and was one of the only adults who knew about the kids' secret detective agency.

"Hold up." Matt held up his hand, even though Jack couldn't see him. "Some football dude hid a buried treasure? Totally cool. Especially since San Francisco is, like, the best team ever."

Steve rolled his eyes, slightly annoyed with his friend. "Seriously, Matt, you need to pay more attention at school. Forty-niner is the nickname they gave to men who moved to northern California to hunt for gold during the gold rush of eighteen *forty-nine*. That's what Jack's referring to, not some sports team."

"Oh," Matt said, then shrugged. He reached for a piece of chocolate in the candy dish next to the phone on the coffee table. "Whatever. It's still a good name for a football team."

Jenny threw a pillow at him. "Anyway, Jack," she said, "tell us more about the treasure."

"The museum in Shakesville has the whole story. The way I understand it, a man named Josiah Carney moved there in the heat of the gold rush, hit a mother lode, then got sick and died, leaving behind a note that supposedly told people where to find the hidden gold. Thousands of treasure-seekers tried, but no one ever found anything. Most people decided the note was a hoax, something he did as a joke, and gave up on the search."

Steve's enthusiasm grew. "Where's the note now?"

"In the museum. As soon as I heard the story, I knew if anyone could find that gold, it'd be the three of you. So, if you're interested—"

"We're definitely interested," Steve interrupted.

Jack laughed. "I figured as much. There's a couple of trailers on the lot that you guys can bunk in, but there is one small catch…I need to use you guys as extras occasionally. I couldn't exactly tell my director that I'm bringing you all out here to hunt for treasure, so I told him you three had worked with me before, and that you were very reliable kids. It also helps that he's met Jenny's dad."

"OMG. You mean we get to hunt for treasure *and* be in a movie?" Jenny clapped her hands. "This is, like, a dream come true."

"I'll email you the paperwork about the movie," Jack said, "so you can get permission from your parents."

At four o'clock that afternoon, the three kids stood on a platform in Beachdale waiting for the train to take them to Sacramento. Steve pushed a bead of sweat from his forehead up into his slight afro, wondering if he brought enough sunscreen for his dark skin. "Jack said he'll be at the station waiting for us when we get there."

Jenny tied her long blonde hair into a pony tail. "OMG, I'm so excited. A treasure hunt and a movie set!"

Matt swallowed the last bite of his granola bar, then wadded the wrapper into a ball and tossed it into the nearby trash can. "And you know what the best part is? No ghosts. No psycho-killers with guns. This might be the first treasure we've gone

3

after where no one's actually gonna try to kill us or scare us off."

The train arrived, and the trio clambered on board, discussing the various ways they would spend the treasure. An hour and a half later, they arrived at the station in Sacramento and found Jack waiting for them, as promised.

"Hope you guys aren't in too much of a hurry, the movie set is still over an hour's drive."

"Will there be food when we get there?" Matt asked.

Jack chuckled. "I forgot about that appetite of yours. Good to see some things never change." He glanced at his watch. "Yeah, we'll probably catch the tail end of the dinner buffet if we hurry."

Matt hurled his suitcase inside the open trunk of the car, then tossed Jenny's and Steve's bags inside, and slammed the trunk shut. "Let's go!" He flung the back door open and jumped inside. Laughing, Steve and Jenny climbed in after him.

"Tell us about the movie," Jenny said as the car merged onto the freeway.

"Well," Jack began, "it's an action thriller about two guys on the run from the police. The scenes we're filming now are when the main characters end up in a small town, hiding in a barn while their car is being fixed by the local mechanic. We're only in Shakesville for another few days, then we pack up and move to Sacramento."

Steve nodded slowly. "Which means we've only got a few days to find that treasure."

Leaning back, Jenny flipped her hair to the side. "Which will be no problem for the Decoders."

"Okay if we eat first?" Matt rubbed his belly. "No way am I gonna be useful on an empty stomach."

Steve noticed Jenny's blue eyes twinkle and a smile spread across her face. "Technically," she said, "you aren't really useful with a full stomach either."

Matt threw her an evil look. "At least I—"

"Tell us more about the treasure," Steve interrupted before his two friends began to argue pointlessly like they always did. "Is the gold supposed to be in coins or bars or what?"

Jack shrugged. "To tell you the truth, I don't know the specifics about it. The museum can give you more details. They'll be open tomorrow at nine."

For the remainder of the ride, they discussed the movie and the different scenes that would require the kids to stand in as extras.

When they arrived at the set, Jack escorted them to their trailers. "I'm afraid these aren't quite as nice as the ones you stayed in last time, but at least they're next to each other."

The group walked into the boys' trailer first, which Steve noticed had two twin beds separated by a small, wooden nightstand. Matt and Steve put their suitcases down and then followed Jenny next door into her trailer, which had only one bed and a small loveseat with a nightstand between the two which held a candy dish full of chocolate.

"These are perfect," Jenny said as she rolled her suitcase next to her bed. "I mean, it's not like we're gonna be in here much, anyway."

Matt rubbed his hands together. "You said something about a dinner buffet?"

Jack grinned. "I guess I better show you guys the mess tent before Matt passes out."

As they walked toward dinner, Steve took a quick survey of the area. Several trailers dotted the outskirts of the set. Toward the middle was a large fake front of a barn, which Steve knew in the movie industry to be called a façade, and farther away stood more fake fronts made to look like the main center of a town.

Jack pointed to the facades. "We're only shooting the outside scenes here. All the inside shots were done back in the studio in Burbank, that's why we don't need the full buildings."

"And the actors?" Jenny looked around. "Are they staying here, too?"

Jack shook his head. "The main actors don't get here until the day after tomorrow. Till then, we're just shooting the background shots and the stunts."

Jenny's shoulders slumped a little and Steve

knew she was disappointed. She followed the movie scene very carefully and he imagined meeting the actors in person would've made her whole year.

As they approached the food tents, the smell of bar-b-que overpowered everything. Matt sniffed the air and his eyes closed. "Aw, dudes, I am in heaven."

Jack motioned for them to grab plates. "Help yourselves. I've got some things to work on, but you all feel free to roam around the set. Just don't break anything." He paused. "But then again, if you did break something, you've got Miss Fix-Anything here to help you out."

Jenny beamed. Her dad owned a repair shop, and after helping him out many times, she had become great at fixing things herself.

Matt grabbed a plate. "The only thing I plan on breaking is the world record for rib-eating."

After saying goodbye to Jack, the three friends loaded their plates with food and found an empty table to sit at. Jenny opened her cornbread muffin and smeared honey on it. "What should we do when we're done eating?"

Steve wiped bar-b-que sauce off the side of his mouth. "Go exploring. What else?"

"Mind if we sit with you guys?" a man said.

Steve looked up and saw two men in their early thirties motioning toward the empty seats next to the kids.

Matt nodded. "It's all good."

"Thanks." The taller of the two men sat down next to Matt. His brown hair was cropped military-style and his clothes had a few tears in them. "I'm Grant Anderson and this is Brian Metcalf. We're stunt doubles on the set."

Brian, whose blond hair hung down to his shoulders, sat beside Steve and gave them a short wave. "How's it going?"

"Good," Matt said before shoveling a giant spoonful of baked beans into his mouth.

Steve swallowed a quick sip of soda. "I'm Steve Kemp, and these are my friends, Matt Peterson and Jenny Reed."

"Nice to meet you guys," Grant said. "I haven't seen you around before. Did you just get here?"

Jenny nodded. "Yeah, literally, like ten minutes ago. We're extras in a couple of the scenes coming up."

After unrolling the utensils from the napkin, Grant began to cut into his chicken. "That's cool. They have a nice museum in town if you get bored. There's some interesting stuff from the gold mining days to look at."

"Yeah," Brian said. "There's even a treasure map."

"A treasure map?" Steve threw Matt and Jenny a warning look. "That sounds interesting. What kind of treasure map?"

Grant smiled. "An old miner supposedly hid a treasure and left a note as a challenge for someone to find it. If you're smart enough to figure out where it is, you'll be rich."

"Yeah," Brian said and chuckled. "Just watch out for the ghost."

Matt choked on a potato chip and began coughing. He rubbed his chest, then reached for his can of cola.

"Are you okay?" Jenny asked, patting his back.

Matt took a few sips and nodded, then pushed her hand away. "Yeah, I'm okay. Did you just say ghost?"

Brian chuckled again. "According to the museum, the ghost of the miner is still out there, protecting his treasure from anyone who might want to steal it."

"But, if he left a note for people to find it," Steve said and frowned, "why would he be trying to keep people from taking it? That seems illogical."

Grant shrugged. "Exactly. It's just a crazy story. But the note is still pretty cool to look at, even if the old man was insane."

A blonde woman in her twenties sat down at the table next to Grant. "Hey, big guy. Missed you at lunch."

"Sorry, Peg. Had to skype with my son." He pointed to the kids. "These three just joined us on set. Kids, this is Peggy Ayers."

9

"Hi, guys. Welcome to the set."

"Thanks," Jenny said. "Are you a stunt double, too?"

She laughed. "No way. Have you seen the crazy things these knuckleheads do? I'm a camera gal. That's my thing."

"We were just telling the kids about the hidden treasure," Grant said.

"And the ghost," Brian added.

Peggy shook her head. "I hope you kids aren't thinking about going after the treasure. You know what happened to the last guys who tried it, don't you?"

Matt gulped. "Wh…what happened to them?"

She looked around as though making sure no one was listening. "They set out one morning to look for the gold, then," she paused, leaned her head in, and lowered her voice, "they gave up and came back for lunch."

She burst into laughter. "Sorry, kids, I couldn't resist. But seriously, don't go out into the desert on a wild goose chase. There are rattlesnakes and wolves out there. It could be dangerous."

"For Pete's sake," Grant said. "Stop mothering them, Peg. They'll be fine."

A tall man with salt-and-pepper hair and matching neatly trimmed beard walked up to the table. "Sorry to interrupt dinner, but Stan needs to see you three in his office, pronto."

Grant sighed and put down his fork. "Never a moment's rest."

Peggy stood. "That's the breaks when you're the best."

Once the adults left, Jenny turned to her friends. "Did you hear that? A ghost is protecting the treasure. OMG, this is getting better and better!"

Matt gripped his over-stuffed pulled-pork sandwich. "Dudes, can we please not talk about ghosts while I'm eating?"

Jenny reached for her soda. "Well, I guess that means we can never talk about ghosts again."

Matt scowled, his mouth full of food. "Hmmph, hmmph, hmmph." His fake laugh came out muffled.

Grinning, Jenny dipped a French fry in ketchup.

As Steve pushed baked beans around his plate with a fork, he contemplated the rumor of a ghost protecting the gold. The thought intrigued him. "I wonder what the real story is behind the miner's treasure."

"Aww, dang it!" Matt wiped spilled bar-b-que sauce on his shirt with his napkin and ended up smearing it around even worse. Finally, he shrugged and threw the napkin down. "Jack said the museum opens at nine. We'll find out then." He took another bite of his sandwich and more pulled pork plopped onto his shirt.

Jenny grabbed a clean napkin, opened it, and

tucked it into the top of Matt's shirt like a bib. "You seriously should do this like every time you eat."

Steve put his fork down and set his jaw. "I don't want to wait until morning."

Matt groaned. "Dude, please tell me we're not gonna break into the museum tonight. We just got here and you're already planning a breaking-and-entering job. And I haven't even eaten dessert yet."

Steve pulled out his cell. "Relax, Matt. I don't intend to break into anything. I just meant that we can ask Alysha to look it up for us and see what she finds out tonight. That way, when we get to the museum tomorrow, we'll already have some background knowledge about the treasure."

Jenny half-smiled as she looked at Steve. "So, we're using the treasure as an excuse to call Alysha this time? That's cool. I'm *sure* she won't mind."

Steve felt his face get hot. Alysha Stonestreet was a whiz on the internet and had helped the Decoders out on all their missions. She also had a huge crush on Steve, something Jenny loved teasing him about.

"Hey, Alysha," Steve said once the girl answered. "It's Steve. You're on speakerphone."

"Hi, Alysha!" Jenny added.

"Mmfh, mmfh." Matt pointed at his mouth.

"That was Matt," Jenny said, "with his mouth full of food, as usual."

Alysha laughed. "Hey, guys. What's up?"

"Think you could do the Decoders a favor?" Steve asked.

"Sure. What do you need?"

Steve and Jenny, with occasional interjections from Matt, explained everything they had heard so far about the treasure, including the possibility of a ghost.

"Yeah, no problem," Alysha said. "But I can't get to it until tomorrow. We've got some family friends coming over tonight so I'm kinda busy."

"No worries," Steve said. "Just whenever you get a chance."

Once the trio finished eating and threw their trash away, they began their exploration of the movie set, starting with the façade of the town. Each "building" had an elaborate front, complete with benches, flower pots, and even a fake sidewalk.

Matt walked behind one of the fronts made to look like a general store. "Dudes, it's so awesome how this totally looks like a real town and then you walk behind and they're just wooden frames held up by beams."

"Right?" Jenny said. "I think the movie industry is like *the* most amazing thing on the planet. Nothing is ever what it seems."

As the trio stood examining the backs of the fake buildings, voices approached from the front. Steve put his finger to his lips motioning for the other two to be quiet. He was pretty sure it was okay for them to be back there, but he didn't want to take any chances, not on their first day.

"I don't know, Sam," a man said. "With what's been happening, maybe we should call the cops."

Steve perked up. What could be going on that they needed to call the police?

"No," Sam replied. "No cops. We definitely don't need the fuzz snooping around out here. We've come too far to risk getting caught. Hold on. Here they come. We'll talk more about this later."

Steve wanted desperately to see who the two men were. He snuck as quietly as he could to the end of the fake building and peeked. Too late. A crowd of people stood around talking, making it impossible to know which two of the men he had heard speaking.

Afraid he would be noticed and then suspected of eavesdropping, Steve motioned for his friends to follow him. They walked all the way down the backsides of the fake town until they reached the end, then walked away from the crowd. Nobody seemed to notice them.

As they made their way to their trailers, Matt said, "That was weird, right?"

Jenny nodded. "Totally. Did you hear what the guy named Sam said? OMG. He doesn't want to call the cops because he's afraid they'll get caught, so whatever they're doing, it's gotta be illegal."

Steve chewed on his lip. "But, the first guy brought up calling the police because of what's been happening, which obviously has nothing to do with their criminal undertakings."

"*Criminal undertakings?*" Matt repeated and grinned. "Dude, you've been watching way too many crime shows."

Steve rolled his eyes. Considered a nerd by most, Steve occasionally used big words and his friends loved to tease him for it. "Anyway, whatever the case, there's something going on here, something bad, and I intend to find out what."

2 MYSTERIOUS FOOTPRINTS

Steve followed his friends inside Jenny's trailer, took a quick look behind him to make sure no one had followed them, and then closed the door.

"So, what's our first move?" Jenny asked after jumping onto the bed.

Steve sat on the sofa next to Matt. "I suggest we talk to Jack and tell him everything we overheard. He can tell us if there's something going on. And if he's not aware of anything, then maybe he can start keeping an eye out for him. This Sam guy and his cohort are obviously doing something bad. Perhaps we can help find out what."

Yawning, Matt stretched his arms up over his head. "Think maybe we can tell him in the morning, dude? I'm bushed. And remember, breakfast starts real early out here."

"And no way would we want to miss that,"

Jenny said, grinning. "Matt would probably start to cry."

Steve laughed. On their second case, the kids had been hired as extras for a movie and stayed on location as well. Matt's biggest grudge was how early they had to get up for breakfast, but, he never passed up the opportunity for food.

After bidding goodnight to Jenny, the boys walked over to their trailer and got ready for bed. As Steve lay staring at the ceiling, something bothered him. The two men they overheard were into something shady, something they didn't want to get caught doing and didn't want anyone else to know about. So, what could possibly be going on that would make one of them even contemplate calling the police? It had to be something major. But what?

At six o'clock the next morning, Steve followed Matt and Jenny toward the mess tent, his mind still on the conversation they had overheard.

Matt yawned. "Seriously, dudes, I could never work in the movie industry. Can you imagine getting up this early every day?"

"But think of how great the food is," Jenny pointed out. "Wouldn't that alone be worth it?"

Matt teetered his head back and forth as if weighing the options. "I'm gonna have to think about that when my stomach's not growling."

"So, we're basically never gonna get an answer," Jenny said.

They reached the beginning of the buffet line and the smell of cooked bacon filled the air. Because the morning shoot began at seven, the mess tent was packed. Once they had filled their plates, they saw Jack waving them over.

As the three friends sat at the table, Jack reached for his giant cup of coffee. "Did you kids get a good night's sleep?"

Steve nodded. "Yeah, thanks. The beds are very comfortable." He glanced around to make sure no one could hear him, then told Jack about the conversation they overheard.

After listening carefully to the story, he frowned. "That's very strange."

"Is there anything bad going on?" Steve asked. "Something we can help look into?"

Jack shook his head. "No, nothing. In fact, everything has been going great. We're even ahead of schedule."

Steve cut into the giant slice of ham on his plate. "The guy named Sam said they didn't need cops snooping around. If you point out who Sam is, then perhaps we can keep an eye on him and see if we can figure out if he's into anything shady."

Leaning back, Jack crossed his arms. "That's the strange part. There's no one named Sam working on the set."

Steve arched an eyebrow, surprised. "No one?"

"Maybe it's a nickname," Matt suggested. "You know, like my real name's Matthew but everyone calls me Matt."

Jack stroked his chin. "I can't think of anyone. There's no Sam, Samuel, Sampson, or anything close. Whoever you heard talking last night, they weren't part of the crew."

A heavy-set woman with dark brown hair walked up to them. "Jack, they need you over in wardrobe. Apparently, there's a *crisis* and Amy needs you immediately." Her voice sounded annoyed, as though this kind of thing happened frequently.

Jack sighed. "Duty calls." He stood and lowered his voice. "Listen, I don't need you kids until after lunch. Feel free to look around, but talk to me if you find anything and don't do anything crazy."

Steve nodded. "Understood."

After Jack left, Steve opened his small carton of chocolate milk. "Something very strange is going on."

"I'll say," Matt said. "Did you notice they had chocolate milk but no white milk?"

Ignoring Matt, Steve continued. "Jack said there was no one on the crew named Sam, but the two men we overheard blended into the crowd, so everyone knew them."

Jenny smeared jelly on her toast. "Maybe Sam and his buddy are like, using aliases on set, so everyone knows them by a different name."

"That would explain why Jack didn't recognize the name Sam," Steve said, "and it goes along with their being here doing something shady." He frowned. "What could be happening that would make two imposters so nervous they contemplated calling the police?"

"Hey, guys," Grant said as he and Brian walked up to the table. "Mind if we join you, again?"

"Please do." Jenny moved herself closer to Matt to make room. Brian sat next to her, and Grant sat across from them, next to Steve.

Brian put his plate down and opened his napkin. "What do you guys have going on this morning?"

"We're thinking of checking out the museum," Steve said

Grant nodded. "It's pretty nice. They have a lot of interesting artifacts from the gold rush days, including an old mining car and some weird looking contraptions people invented hoping to get the edge on the competition."

"What are you two doing this morning?" Jenny asked.

Brian took a sip of orange juice. "We're filming a scene in front of the barn. Grant gets to jump off the roof, and I get to wrestle a bull."

"Wrestle a bull?" Matt repeated. "Dude, that does *not* sound fun."

Grant laughed. "It's not a real bull. I actually wrestle a mannequin bull and they CGI a real bull in later."

"OMG, that is so cool!" Jenny said. "I love the way they make those scenes look so realistic in the final film."

Brian nodded. "Yeah, those tech guys are the real deal."

"Good morning, gentlemen." Peggy sat down next to Grant. "And you too, kids. How was your first night here?"

"Good," Jenny said, reaching for her orange juice. "The beds are like, super comfy."

"That's nice," Peggy said, but looked as though she had something else on her mind. "Grant, when you're done, can you stop by the trailer? There's something I want you to see."

He nodded. "Sure."

"Thanks." She stood. "Have a good day, kids."

Brian pointed his fork at her as she walked off. "Okay, that was weird. She's usually way more talkative than that."

Grant gave a short laugh. "I know. Usually, we can't get her to shut up."

The kids chatted with the stunt doubles for a while until the two adults left to prepare for their scene. Steve glanced at his watch. "It's only seven.

The museum doesn't open for a couple of hours. Feel like doing some more exploring?"

"Um, yeah!" Jenny jumped up and grabbed her trash, then moved toward the nearby garbage can. Matt and Steve followed.

More active than the previous evening, the movie set teemed with people everywhere.

"Where should we go?" Matt asked.

Steve stopped and took a quick survey of the entire set. "Let's go to the edge and walk the perimeter. That way we'll have a better idea of the size of the site and everything around it."

The other two agreed and soon they arrived at a dirt road leading away from the set. Jenny pointed off in the distance. "That must be the town where the museum is."

Steve studied it for a moment. "It doesn't look too far away. What do you think, Matt?"

Matt squinted toward the town. "About a mile and a half. It'll probably only take about twenty minutes to get there."

"Good," Jenny said. "That gives us plenty of time to explore before the museum opens."

As the kids began their search of the premises, they discovered that the set had three distinct sections: the main movie set with the barn and the façade of the town, the trailer area with not only the cast's trailer's, but also wardrobe, props, and make-up, and the third section comprised of the office trailers as well as the mess tent. The entire area was only a little over a square mile.

Once they returned to where they started, Jenny glanced at her cell phone. "Well, that didn't take too long. Now what?"

Matt stretched his arms up over his head. "How about a nap?"

"Or," Steve said, "I noticed a small dirt path over near the barn setup. Let's see where it goes."

"I don't know about that," Matt said. "Remember what Peggy said about rattlesnakes and wolves?"

Steve headed in the direction of the barn. "Wolves only come out at night, and rattlesnakes tend to avoid activity and are mainly dangerous if you taunt them. So, as long as we're careful and stay on the path, we should be fine."

"I'm game," Jenny said.

"That's what I'm afraid of." Matt chuckled. "Get it? Game? As in, hunting? Rattlesnakes hunt their *game*." He burst out laughing at his own joke.

Jenny groaned and Steve just shook his head. Still snickering, Matt followed his friends toward the small dirt path to begin their quest into the desert.

As the sun began to climb in the sky, Matt wiped some sweat off his forehead. "You know, dudes, I'm not sure this is such a great idea to come out here without water."

Steve rubbed his own forehead with the back of his arm. "I think you're right."

"That'll be a first," Jenny said.

"Ha, ha," Matt said. "At least I—"

"Stop!" Steve interrupted.

Matt and Jenny froze.

"What is it?" Matt said, his voice slightly quavering. "A rattlesnake? A wolf? A bear?"

"No." Steve pointed to the ground in front of them. "Footprints."

Matt put his hand on his heart. "Dude, don't scare me like that."

Kneeling, Steve examined the prints in the sand which looked to be large and fairly deep. "Matt, make your footprint next to this one."

Matt obeyed and Steve studied the comparison. "Whoever made these was definitely heavier and bigger than Matt."

"Well, that narrows it down to all the men on the set," Matt mumbled.

Steve rolled his eyes. "Let me finish. He's heavier and bigger than Matt, but look at how close together the footprints are."

Jenny walked alongside the tracks. "You're right. His steps are way smaller than even mine."

"So it's a big guy who takes tiny steps." Matt shrugged. "What's the big deal?"

"Nothing yet, but it is unusual." Steve stood. "Okay, I say we call it quits. It's getting hot."

The others agreed and the trio began their walk back toward the movie set. Suddenly, Steve stopped. "Hold on." He knelt on the ground. "Check this out. It's the same footprints, only this time, they're *crossing* ours."

After lowering himself next to Steve and looking at the prints, Matt stood back up. "Maybe we just walked over them earlier and didn't notice them."

"No." Steve pointed. "Look closer. The footprints are *on top* of ours."

Jenny frowned. "But, that means whoever it is was just here like two minutes ago."

They looked around. Nothing.

"Okay," Matt said. "I'm getting a little freaked out."

"Do you think someone's stalking us?" Jenny asked as she glanced around again.

Steve shook his head slowly. "Let's not overthink this. We're fairly close to the movie set. People probably walk around all the time." He could tell his voice did not sound as convincing as his words.

"How about we get some water and then head over to the museum?" Matt suggested.

Neither of the other two objected. As they headed toward the mess hall for some bottled water, Steve thought about the mysterious footprints. Although it did seem unlikely that anyone would be following them, he had an uneasy feeling about it. And his feelings were rarely wrong.

3 THE MINER'S NOTE

Steve opened the door to the museum and saw a gray-haired docent with a name badge that read *Christopher* walking up to them.

"Welcome to the Shakesville Museum," he said. "Let me know if you have any questions."

After thanking the man, the three friends wandered around, admiring all the exhibits, especially the strange collection of inventions created to make mining easier. Matt pointed to one that resembled a flowerpot but had multiple holes all around it. "Dude, this one looks like a giant tub of swiss cheese. What do you think it was used for?"

Steve scratched his chin. "I'm going to guess gold panning. They probably filled the pot with dirt and then flushed it out with water through the holes hoping the gold would stay inside."

"Think it worked?" Matt asked.

Steve shrugged. "Considering it's in the section of the museum called *unusual contraptions*, I'm presuming not."

"Guys!" Jenny called from across the room. "Over here."

As the boys walked up, she pointed to a piece of paper encased in a large display case.

"This is it," she said, excitement in her voice. "This is the miner's note."

"Ah," the museum docent's voice cut into their conversation. "I see you've found our greatest mystery."

"Yes, sir," Steve said. "Could you tell us about it? A couple of the men on the movie set mentioned it to us."

The elderly man smiled and inhaled a deep breath. "Legend has it that back in eighteen forty-nine, at the height of the gold rush, a miner named Josiah Carney came into town, sick as a dog, and checked himself into the local hotel. The town doctor paid him a visit and determined that the poor miner was dying and didn't have much time left. Josiah then asked for paper and a quill, and wrote down the note you see in this case."

Steve moved his head down to get a better look at the note. "The men who told us about it said it was a treasure map."

"That it is," the docent said. "According to

Josiah, he had spent the last month accumulating a mound of treasure that he planned to haul back east. Once he started getting sick, he realized he had to hide it in order to seek medical attention. When he found out he was dying, he decided to leave a note, a treasure map if you will, leading to the hidden treasure."

"And?" Matt prompted.

"And, there it is in front of you. Many people have tried to decipher the note, but all have failed." The man chuckled. "Perhaps you three will have better luck."

After studying the note intently, Steve frowned. "How did people know he was telling the truth? He could've just made up the story as a way to get attention before he died."

The man crossed his arms. "Here's where the story gets a bit more interesting. Josiah had a bag with him in his hotel room. Now, at the time, everyone assumed the bag to be full of clothes, but once the sick man died, the doctor opened the bag and found it full of gold nuggets, enough to make any man rich."

Matt whistled. "And Josiah said he had even more of it hidden."

"A mound if it," Jenny added.

Something about the story compelled Steve, even more than just the thought of hidden treasure. There was something about the man himself, Josiah, that intrigued him. "What did he die of? I mean, what was the diagnosis of his illness?"

"According to the doctor, Josiah had what they called consumption. Today, it's called tuberculosis. He also had severe hip problems, possibly a result of all the mining. It affected his walking."

Jenny frowned. "If he couldn't walk, then how did he get to town?"

"He could walk," the elderly man said, "but the pain in his hips caused him to take very small steps."

That caught Steve's attention. "Was he a big man?"

The docent nodded. "Quite big. And heavy. It took three men to carry his body down to the morgue."

Steve looked at his two friends and could tell by their expressions they were all thinking the same thing: small steps from a large, heavy man...those were the footsteps they had found out in the desert.

"Would it be okay if we take a picture of it with our phones?" Steve asked.

The man motioned toward the display case. "Help yourself. But, the writing is pretty faded now. We have replicas for sale in the gift shop. They're easier to read than the note itself."

"Thank you," Steve said. "We'll check that out before we leave."

When another museum guest waved the docent

over, Steve whipped out his phone. "We should all take pictures of this to compare later."

"Why not just buy the replica?" Matt asked.

"I plan to." Steve snapped a few pictures. "But it may be helpful to have pics of the original, too."

Matt took out his cell. "If you say so."

After completing their tour of the museum, they stopped by the gift shop where each kid bought a replica and Jenny bought a small snow globe of the town. As they walked back toward the set, Matt pointed to the bag in Jenny's hand. "Jenn, seriously, what are you gonna do with that thing?"

She held the bag up to her heart. "OMG, I love this thing! Don't you think the name of the town is like the coolest name ever?"

"You like the name Shakesville for a town?" Steve frowned. "You know it was named that because of the number of earthquakes the people here experienced."

"Yeah," Jenny said, "but it's still a cool name. It sounds so…historical."

Matt tossed up his hands dramatically. "That's what the town name means? Are you kidding me? I thought they named it that because this is where you can find the best triple-chocolate shakes in the world."

Steve chuckled, but Jenny rolled her eyes. "Ugh," she said. "Why does everything that comes out of your mouth have to do with food?"

Matt grinned. "It's not just what comes out, but what goes in."

"Why do I even talk to you?" Jenny stomped her feet.

Steve grabbed both their arms, pulling them to a stop.

"What?" Matt said. "We're just joking around."

Steve pointed ahead of them. Black flumes of smoke rose into the air.

"Holy smokes!" Matt said. "The movie set is on fire!"

The three kids broke into a run.

As they neared the location, they slowed down. People had gathered around, observing the fire, but no one seemed the least bit concerned.

Steve spotted Brian over to the side and ran up to him. "What happened?"

"They just filmed the fire scene." Then, apparently noticing the concerned look on the kids' faces, he added, "It wasn't a real fire. It's part of the movie."

Matt placed a hand over his heart. "Dude, that almost gave me a heart attack."

Brian opened his arms wide and grinned. "Welcome to the movies, where nothing is as it seems."

While Peggy and another camera operator moved the cameras around the flames, several crewmen stood nearby preparing to put out the fire.

"Well," Brian said, "I'm off to film my next stunt. You guys have fun today."

"Thanks," Steve said and watched the man walk off.

"I sure am glad that wasn't a real fire," Matt said.

"Right?" Jenny said. "That would've been awful."

Steve pointed into the crowd of crew members. "There's Jack. Let's go see how everything's going."

Since Jack appeared to be in the middle of a serious conversation, the kids waited at a distance to not interrupt. Soon, Jack waved them over. "Kids, I'd like you to meet Michael Anderson, he's our special effects guy."

"Nice to meet you," Steve said. "I'm Steve Kemp, and these are my friends, Matt Peterson and Jenny Reed."

"Welcome to the set." Michael shook each of their hands. "I hear you're the kids in this afternoon's scene."

Jenny clapped her hands. "Yes! And, OMG, we are so excited."

Michael laughed. "Glad to hear it. Well, Jack, I'll catch up with you later. I've got to see if Brian's ready to be set on fire."

"Set on fire?" Matt repeated.

Michael nodded. "Yeah, the main character

Rizzo catches fire in the explosion you just saw, so now we need to film Brian on fire, so we can put it out."

"Is that safe?" Matt asked.

"Of course. We take a million precautions to make sure nothing goes wrong. Trust me, I've done this dozens of times."

Once the man left, Steve turned to Jack. "How's everything going?"

"Great, so far. Everything seems to be going according to plan. What have you three been up to?"

"We just came back from the museum," Steve answered.

Jack glanced at his cell phone. "It's pretty neat, isn't it?"

Jenny nodded. "There was a lot of cool stuff in there."

After checking his cell again, Jack looked up. "Did you see the miner's note?"

"Saw it, took pictures of it, bought the replica." Matt said.

Jack laughed. "Perfect! Now you're ready to hunt for treasure. Well, almost ready. After lunch today, I need the three of you to head over to the wardrobe trailer and then to make-up. It shouldn't take too long to get you ready. We'll start filming your scene around two."

"Sounds good," Steve said.

Sighing, Jack checked his phone yet again. "All right, I've got to get back to work. See you all in a little while."

After he left, Jenny turned to her friends. "Now what?"

Steve replied, "I say we get back to the room and check out what the miner's note says."

"Sounds good to me," Matt said, "and then...lunch!"

The kids relocated to Jenny's trailer where the boys sat on the sofa and Jenny on her bed. All three pulled up the photos of the note on their cells.

Using her fingers to enlarge the image, Jenny stared at the screen. "It's really hard to make out exactly what the words say. I'm glad we bought the replicas." She put down her phone, pulled the replica out of a bag, then placed the snow globe on the nightstand.

Steve squinted at the image on his own phone. Many of the words were faded and difficult to make out. "Why don't you read it out loud? I'm going to attempt to follow along on the original."

Jenny cleared her throat. "*If you're reading this, then I be dead and the gold waits for you. Find the fountain and bathe in it to be clean before the journey. Then you can walk away and go to the land of flowers. Choose the rosiest and smell it hard. Then the real work begins. Squeeze like a lemon and then roll like dough. If you make it through the pipes, you're almost there. All you need is a shovel.*"

Matt reached into the candy dish on the nightstand for a piece of chocolate. "Well, I'm starting to see why no one's ever found the treasure."

"It sounds like gibberish," Jenny said.

Steve pulled on his lower lip. "We're going to need some time to figure this out." His phone beeped and he checked the text. "It's Alysha. I texted her the information we found out at the museum. She wants us to call her."

"Good timing," Jenny said.

Steve called their friend who answered the phone, "Hi, Steve."

"Hey, Alysha, you're on speakerphone." He placed his cell on the couch. "Did you find out anything about the miner and the so-called ghost?"

"Yeah, I did. Although I'm not sure how much you're going to like it. Especially you, Matt."

"Oh, great," Matt said.

"Okay, here it is. Your miner's name is, as you know, Josiah Carney. But that's not his real name."

"What do you mean?" Jenny asked.

"I mean that he was actually born Jeremiah Cabalt, and he's from Virginia. He changed his name when he moved to California, which by the way, he did in eighteen forty-three, when California still belonged to Mexico."

"Interesting." Steve jotted notes down on a sheet of paper, then made a mental note to transfer them to his phone later. "If he didn't move to California for the gold rush, then do we know why he moved here?"

"Uh-huh," Alysha answered. "He was a blacksmith. He got into trouble with the law in Virginia and escaped on a Spanish ship which took him to San Diego. He continued to work as a blacksmith until the gold rush began, then he moved up to northern California to try his fortune."

"Which he allegedly made," Steve said. "What else do we know about him? Do we know what got him into trouble in Virginia?"

"No, but it must have been something pretty bad because I found a reward poster offering five hundred dollars for his return."

"That was a lot of money for back then," Steve commented. "Anything else?"

Alysha continued. "You already know the part about him getting really sick, but what you don't know, is that before he got sick, he had a partner, a man named Allen Jacobs. The two of them supposedly went in on the equipment together but then had a major falling out."

"What happened to this Jacobs dude?" Matt reached for another piece of chocolate.

"From what I found out, he died in San Francisco a few years after Josiah. Some people think the note Josiah left behind was intended for Jacobs, and that only he would know what the note meant."

Steve stopped writing and bit his lip. "If that's true, then the more we know about Allen Jacobs the better prepared we'll be to decipher the note. Could you find out everything you can about Allen Jacobs?"

"Uh-huh. But it won't be till tonight. I've got family stuff going on this afternoon."

"That's cool," Steve said.

"But wait," Alysha said. "I'm not done with the story. I haven't told you about the ghost yet."

Matt groaned. "I was hoping you were going to forget about that."

Alysha laughed. "No such luck. After Josiah died, the doctor found the gold in his bag along with the note, like you guys already know, but what you don't know is what happened to Josiah's body."

"Do we really need to know?" Matt said. "Because this already sounds creepy."

"Shh," Jenny said. "Go on, Alysha."

"The doctor sent his body down to the morgue, where they did an autopsy. The next morning, the body disappeared."

Matt gulped. "Disappeared? How does a body just...disappear?"

"It doesn't," Steve said. "There's a logical explanation for it. Somebody took his body."

"But, why?" Jenny asked. "Why would anyone want a dead body?"

"There is another explanation," Alysha said.

"What's that?" Jenny asked.

"The body walked away."

Matt held up his hands even though Alysha couldn't see him. "Okay. I'm done. The miner's a zombie? That's it. I am officially through with this case."

Alysha laughed. "Not a zombie, Matt. I found several reports of people who swear they saw Josiah walking through town the next day. And even more reports of people who swear they saw him roaming the desert. That's where the rumor about his ghost comes from. Except, the reports didn't say he was a ghost, they say it was him, in the flesh, looking exactly as he did before he died, all pale from consumption and walking with the crippled short steps from his hip problems."

Steve scrunched his forehead in thought. "Could it be that the doctor was mistaken about his death?"

"No," Alysha said. "The coroner conducted an autopsy. The guy was definitely dead."

Matt shook his head. "This is just too weird. It's not a ghost out there protecting his treasure, it's the actual dude. The dead dude. The dead, came back to life because he's a zombie, dude."

"Did you find out anything else, Alysha?"

Steve asked, deciding to ignore Matt's ramblings.

"Only that Josiah had one daughter, but I couldn't find any evidence of descendants still alive."

"So, there's no one to rightfully claim the treasure?" Steve said.

"Yep," Alysha said. "It's basically finders, keepers."

"And we intend to be the finders," Jenny said.

Just then, a loud bell sounded outside.

Matt closed his eyes and inhaled a deep breath. "Music to my ears."

"The lunch bell just rang," Jenny said. "We better go before Matt turns into a zombie himself."

Alysha chuckled. "Okay. I'll do some more digging tonight and let you guys know what I find out."

"Thanks," Steve said and hung up. He leaned back into the sofa and crossed his arms. If the miner's body had indeed disappeared, who would've taken it? It could've been his ex-partner, but he wouldn't have been able to do it alone; it took three men to carry the body to the morgue. And, why would he take the body in the first place? Steve sighed. The more they learned about the case, the more confusing it became.

4 LOST!

As they left for lunch, Steve's thoughts continued to focus on the miner. If his partner, Allen Jacobs, had come back, he would have seen the note, and if it was truly meant for him, then he would have deciphered it and found the gold. But he didn't. Why not? Did he not know about the note and the gold? Or, did he know, but just couldn't figure it out?

The smell of fried rice and egg rolls drifted through the air.

Matt picked up a paper plate and utensils. "Oh, man, I love Chinese food."

"You love all food," Jenny said. "But I have to admit, this does smell amazing."

After piling their plates, they searched for a place to sit and found an empty table at the far end of the tent. As soon as they sat down, several members of the crew joined them so they didn't get a chance to talk about the case like Steve hoped.

They finished eating then headed to the wardrobe trailer where the costume designer gave them flannel shirts to wear over their jeans and boots. In the make-up trailer, the make-up artist applied a minimal amount of powder to the kids' faces and put Jenny's long blonde hair into two French braids.

As they walked out, Matt commented, "Jack was right, that's didn't take long at all."

They approached the set and Jack waved them over. "Perfect timing. I hope none of you are afraid of heights."

"Heights?" Matt repeated.

Jack nodded and led them toward a giant machine that Steve knew to be called a cherry picker. His neighbors rented one every year just after Thanksgiving, so they could reach the top of their house to put up their Christmas lights. The machine was a giant crane with a cage attached at the end.

Jack stopped next to the cherry picker and pointed to the third floor of a three-story building façade. Up at the top, a woman standing on a balcony waved down at the kids.

"That's Marisa," Jack said. "The scene requires the three of you to be with Marisa on that balcony, then, when the director, Mac, gives the cue, you're all going to yell for help. Literally. We want you to yell 'help" over and over again."

"Are we taking the cherry picker to get there?" Steve asked nervously. He had never been in one before, but every time he watched his neighbors get in, it made his stomach queasy.

Jack nodded. "Yeah, sorry about that. There's no stairs out here."

"Hold on a minute." Matt pointed to the cage. "We have to ride this thing? All the way up there?"

Jack chuckled. "Come on now, Matt. Where's your sense of adventure?"

"I'm in," Jenny said and clapped her hands. "It totally looks like fun."

"Once you get there," Jack said, "Marisa will tether you to the building, just in case you get a little…hesitant about the scene."

"You mean just in case we pass out from fright," Matt grumbled.

Jack laughed. "If you don't want to do it, I'll understand. We can always fill in with other extras."

"No, we got this," Jenny said.

Steve got the feeling if he or Matt backed out of being in the movie, Jenny would kill them slowly with a dull spoon. "Yeah," he said and nodded. "We're good."

"Great!" Jack opened the cage of the cherry picker. "In you go."

Jenny climbed in first, followed by Matt and then Steve.

As Jack closed the gate and gave the signal for the operator to begin lifting them, Matt grabbed a hold of the side and muttered to Jenny, "If I die doing this, I'm going to haunt you forever."

"Technically," Jenny said, "if you die, then I would die right beside you, which would make it hard for you to haunt me since I'd be dead, too."

Steve felt his stomach begin to knot up. "Can we not talk about people dying right now?"

"Sorry, dude," Matt said. "Are you okay?"

Steve nodded although he did not at all feel okay. He just wanted it over with as quickly as possible.

When the machine finally reached the balcony, Marisa greeted the kids. "I'm going to have you step out one at a time so I can tether you to the building."

"Is it really that dangerous up here?" Matt asked, a touch of nervousness in his voice.

She shook her head. "Not at all. We just do it as a precaution. Three floors is a long way to fall. Now, who's first?"

"You better go first, Steve," Matt said.

Steve gave a thumbs-up, his stomach still turning from the lift. He stepped onto the balcony and felt Marisa's strong hands grab him and strap a clear harness around him, like the kind parents use on a wandering toddler. Then, she clamped a hook onto the back of his harness.

"You're good to go," she said. "Go ahead and get behind me so I can hook up your friends."

Steve felt better once he was no longer in the cage. He side-stepped to make room for Jenny who came next. Within minutes the three kids stood next to each other overlooking the entire movie set from the top of the balcony.

"It's a super nice view up here," Jenny said. "Think I have time to snap a few pics?"

"Sure," Marisa said. "They'll let us know when they're ready to film. Looks like they're just starting to get in position, so you've got a good four or five minutes."

"Nice!" Jenny whipped out her cell and began taking pictures.

Steve admired the view, especially that of the desert beyond the set. As his eyes became accustomed to the glare of the sun, he noticed something odd. Out in the direction where the kids had gone exploring that morning, there was movement. He squinted and focused his vision. It appeared to be a large man. He turned to say something to Matt, but saw him talking to Marisa. When he turned back, the man had disappeared.

Steve frowned and scanned the area. Nothing. No man. No movement. It was as if he had just vanished into thin air.

"That's the signal," Marisa said. "Get ready to start screaming for help."

Giving up on the man, Steve focused his attention on the scene. When the director gave the cue, the three kids and Marisa began screaming for help and waving their arms. A couple minutes later, they heard someone yell *cut* and they stopped to catch their breath.

Marisa reached down and picked up a walkie-talkie. "How was that?"

A man's voice replied through the speaker, "Good, but we're going to relocate the cameras. Standby for another take."

"Copy that." Marisa put the walkie-talkie back down on the ground. "You guys up for round two?"

"For sure," Jenny said. "This is fun!"

"Yeah," Matt agreed, "I don't really get to scream at the top of my lungs from a balcony too much."

Steve was only half-listening to the conversation. He stared at the desert, trying to get another glimpse of the mysterious large man.

"Looks like they're ready for the next take," Marisa said. "Get ready."

On their cue, the group once again began crying out for help. The scene went a little longer this time and Steve began to feel the strain on his vocal chords.

Finally, they got the signal to stop.

Matt rubbed his throat. "Man, I could really use some ice water right about now."

Marisa picked up the walkie-talkie. "How was that?"

The man on the other end said, "That's going to be fine. They'll come get you guys in a few minutes."

"That's it?" Jenny asked. "We're done?" Her shoulders slumped a little and she seemed disappointed.

"We are, for now. Once we're down, they'll film another scene here for a different part of the movie since they've already got the cameras set up. I don't think they need us again until this evening, but I'll double check."

She pressed the button on the walkie-talkie. "Hey, Zach. When's the next time you need us on set?"

Silence.

"Zach?"

"Sorry about that. I don't need you guys for a while, like maybe around four. Go relax a bit."

She looked at the kids as the cherry picker cage moved toward the balcony. "There you have it. Relax a bit and then plan to meet up with us around four."

"Sounds good," Matt said.

When the cage hit the balcony, Steve cringed and got a little queasy. Jenny climbed in first, followed by Matt, and then Steve went in last. As they moved down toward the ground, Steve felt his stomach tie into knots again. He had no idea why this machine affected him so much. He'd been in much scarier situations, but there was just something about being in a cage up in the air that made him uncomfortable.

When they touched the ground, Steve almost cheered and was the first to get out.

After waving goodbye to Marisa, the trio walked toward their trailers. "So, what now?" Jenny asked.

"Let's go get a drink," Matt said. "My throat needs some serious help."

"I want to go check out that dirt road we were on earlier," Steve said.

"Why?" Matt asked. "There was nothing there."

Steve told them about the man he saw from the balcony.

Matt frowned. "Dude, that could've been anyone from the set."

"I know," Steve said, "but I just have a feeling we need to go back out there."

"Okay," Matt said. "But let's take some water with us this time. It's getting pretty hot out."

"Good idea." Steve agreed.

They walked over to the mess tent and each grabbed a bottled water. After drinking some to alleviate their strained vocal chords, they set off for the trail.

"What should we be looking for?" Matt asked once they started on the dirt path.

Steve glanced around. "I'm not really sure. But someone was out here earlier, and I want to know why."

"Maybe the dude was just looking around, kind of like us," Matt suggested.

"Perhaps," Steve said, "but then where did he go? He literally just disappeared."

They walked for a while in silence, trying to keep their eyes open for any sign of anything strange.

"Hey, guys," Jenny said. "Over here. Check this out." The two boys walked over and she pointed to a set of footprints. "They head off this way, on what kinda looks like a separate path."

"I don't know about this." Matt shook his head. "Heading off a main path doesn't sound like a smart thing to do. What if we get lost?"

Jenny pulled out her phone. "Then we can GPS our way back."

"Does your GPS work out here?" Matt took out his own phone. "I know my internet connection's been spotty ever since we got here."

Jenny punched a few things into her phone. "You're right. My GPS says it's unavailable right now."

Stepping off the main path, Steve kneeled to examine the footprints. "They seem pretty easy to follow. Worst case scenario, we find nothing and follow the footprints back to this spot." Seeing the hesitation on Matt's face, he continued. "But, no matter what, I don't want to venture off too far. We have to be back in plenty of time for our next scene."

Matt's face relaxed and he glanced at his cell. "How about we agree to go for around fifteen minutes? Then another fifteen minutes will get us back here and we can get to the mess tent in time for a quick snack."

"Perfect," Steve said.

Jenny grinned. "I knew you'd figure out a way to sneak food into our adventure."

Steve took a few steps and motioned to the others. "Come on."

The new path was far less travelled than the previous one, and many times, they had to side-step bushes or jump over large boulders, but the footprints they followed remained clear.

After almost ten minutes, Steve stopped and gestured for the other two to stop as well.

"What's wrong?" Matt asked.

Steve did a quick scan of the area. "The footprints...they just end right here."

"What?" Jenny said and moved herself in front of him.

The footprints simply ended.

"Okay, this is impossible." Steve scowled. "One does not simply stop leaving footprints. Look around, his trail must be here someplace."

They scattered, each examining a different area. After a couple minutes, they regrouped.

"Nothing," Matt said.

"Ditto," Jenny said.

Steve shook his head. "This doesn't make any sense."

"It does if you're a ghost," Matt said.

Steve rolled his eyes. "Matt, there are no such things as ghosts. I think our experience as detectives has taught us that."

"Oh, yeah?" Matt crossed his arms. "You saw a man walking in the desert, then he mysteriously disappeared. We come out here, find his footprints, and guess what? Those mysteriously disappeared, too. So, if there's no such things as ghosts, then you tell me what happened."

"I don't know," Steve admitted. "*Yet*. But there is a logical explanation for all of this. We just have to figure out what it is."

"No," Matt said, "what we need to do is get back to the movie set. I'm getting hungry."

"Um, guys," Jenny's voice cut into their conversation.

"Yeah?" Matt said.

"The footprints, they disappeared," Jenny said.

Matt broke into a laugh. "Wow. Thanks for joining the conversation. What do you think we've been talking about?"

"That's not what I mean." She shook her head slowly. "The footprints, the ones we followed to get here, they're gone."

Steve studied the ground. Jenny was right. The trail of footprints they had followed to get there, as well as their own, had disappeared.

Matt gulped. "Um, so how are we supposed to find our way back?"

The three kids looked at each other and then at their surroundings. They were stuck in the middle of the desert with no idea how to get back, and no one knew where they were.

5 INSIDE THE PROPS SHED

Steve took a quick survey of the area, trying to remain calm. All around, everything looked the same. He pulled out his cell. "No service. How about you two?"

After checking, they both shook their heads.

Suddenly, shots rang through the air.

"Wha...what was that?" Matt said.

Jenny clapped her hands. "Best sound ever! I overheard one of the extras saying they were gonna be doing a shootout scene."

Matt pointed. "The shots came from that direction."

"Follow those shots!" Steve said, feeling a wave of relief. Though he didn't want to admit it, relying on footprints as their only guide back to civilization may not have been the smartest move.

After fifteen minutes of walking, the kids found

the main path and walked quickly back toward the movie set. Once the buildings came into view, they slowed their pace.

"I don't know about you guys," Matt said, "but no way am I going out there again. We were lucky this time."

Steve nodded. "I agree, about the lucky part, that is. Fortunately for all of us, I brought a compass on the trip. It's in the mystery backpack in my suitcase." During their first case, the three kids had created mystery backpacks to take with them whenever they solved mysteries just in case they needed supplies.

"You brought a compass?" Matt repeated. "Seriously? Who even owns a compass?"

"I do," Steve said, "and we could've used it today."

"Totally," Jenny agreed. "I think we should all get them."

Matt conceded. "Yeah, that's probably a good idea, and, not to change the subject or anything, but do you guys wanna head to the mess tent? I think they have chips and stuff."

They both agreed and the trio headed off to get some snacks. As they sat alone at a table munching on chips and soda, Steve thought about the footprints. How could they have just disappeared? If they had been in town, he would've said that the person got into a car or some kind of vehicle. But out here, in the middle of the desert? It didn't make any sense.

As they ate their chips, Grant walked up to them. "Hey, guys. Mind if I join you?"

Matt motioned to the empty seat next to him. "Knock yourself out, dude."

He sat down and began unwrapping a protein bar. "Having a good day so far?"

"Totally." Jenny took a sip of her soda. "We went over to the museum this morning. It was way cool."

"Did you talk to the old guy about the hidden treasure?" Grant asked.

Steve nodded and shot a warning look to the other two. It was best if they kept being investigators a secret. "Yeah. It was pretty interesting."

Grant chuckled. "Let me guess, you all bought the replica miner's note from the gift shop?"

Jenny's eyebrows shot up. "No way! How did you know?"

The stunt double chuckled again. "Because we all have them. Seriously, I think the museum has made more money from the film crew buying those things than they've made all year from everyone else."

"So, a lot of people have the replica note?" Steve bit his lip.

Grant nodded. "Sorry to disappoint you, but

I'm pretty sure everyone has tried to decipher it at some point or other since we got here. But, hey! Maybe you three will be the lucky ones, you never know. Just remember who told you about the treasure when you're rich and famous." He winked.

"For sure, dude." Matt grinned.

Steve played with the empty wrapper in his hands. "Has anyone actually gone out into the desert to look for the treasure?"

Grant shrugged. "If they have, I haven't heard about it. But this schedule keeps us pretty busy. I'm not sure when anyone would actually have time to go treasure hunting." He glanced down at his watch. "Speaking of time, it's almost time for the next scene. I think you guys are in this one, right?"

"Yeah," Jenny said. "Do you know what it's about?"

"It's a short fight scene. The cameras will be outside, focused on the doors of the saloon, then Brian and I come crashing through the doors and into the street where a crowd will gather to watch us fight. I'm guessing you guys are part of the crowd."

"Cool," Matt said. "We get to watch you dudes fight?"

Grant smiled. "Choreographed fighting. It's a pretty short scene, we filmed most of the fight itself already, but we still need to film us crashing through the door."

"What about the regular actors?" Jenny asked.

"The ones you guys are stunt doubling for. Why aren't they here to film it?"

"Gus and Jay will be here tomorrow," Grant explained. "Brian and I just do the stunt part. Once those guys get here, they can film the actual dialogue. I'm guessing they'll need you for that part of the scene, too."

"You mean we'll get to see them in person?" Jenny said, her eyes wide.

Grant laughed. "Yeah, sure. I'll introduce you. They're nice guys."

A woman across the mess tent waved at Grant and motioned for him to join her. He stood. "Looks like I'm being beckoned. I'll catch up with you guys later." He said goodbye and walked off to join the woman.

"Did you hear what he said?" Steve asked.

"Like, O...M...G!" Jenny said. "We get to meet Gus Allen and Jay Wilcox!"

Steve frowned. "I meant about the miner's note."

"You mean how everyone on set has a replica?" Matt said.

Steve nodded. "That means we've got a lot of competition and we need to step up our game."

Matt checked the time on his cell. "Well, before we dive into danger and get lost in the desert again, it's almost four o'clock. We should head down to the set."

After throwing away their trash, the three friends made their way over to the saloon façade. As they approached, Jack waved them over. "Hey, kids. This scene is pretty short. We just need a shot of our stunt doubles crashing through the saloon doors, and we need our extras, including you, to be in the background. Then, tomorrow, we'll film in this same spot but with the actors. I'll need you guys there as well, wearing the exact same thing and with your hair looking exactly the same way. Make-up will help you all with that."

"I can't believe we get to meet Gus Allen and Jay Wilcox," Jenny said. "They're like two of my favorite actors."

Jack nodded. "Yeah, they're pretty fun to work with, too. Not like some other actors."

"You mean like a certain female actor who's always late?" Peggy said as she strolled by.

Jack grunted.

Jenny waited until Peggy walked out of hearing range. "Who was she talking about?"

Jack glanced around as if making sure no one could hear him. "Nancy Mulligan."

"Wait." Matt held up his hand. "Nancy Mulligan is going to be here, too?"

"She's supposed to be," Jack said, "but she's been flaking out on us. She's late for shots; she's forgetting lines. I asked her if everything was okay and she said yes."

"Maybe she's got something going on in her personal life," Matt said. "Something she doesn't want to talk about."

Jenny took a step back and put her hand on her heart. "Matt, are you crushing on Nancy Mulligan? I thought you weren't impressed with celebrities."

Turning a little red in the face, Matt crossed his arms. "I'm not crushing on her; I'm just saying that maybe something's going on that we don't know about."

Jenny pursed her lips. "Oh, well, then maybe you should ask her when she gets here. I'm sure she'll open up to her biggest fan."

"What time are we filming tomorrow?" Steve asked, hoping to distract his friends from an inevitable argument.

Jack smiled at Steve, as if he understood Steve's intentions. "We'll start right around four o'clock, like today. The actors will get here in the late morning, relax a bit, and then we'll start shooting. That one's going to be a longer shoot, so expect to be there well into the evening."

"And in the morning?" Steve asked.

Jack shook his head. "I don't need you in the morning. We've got a scene to film out in the desert at sunrise, but you three aren't in that one."

Matt clasped his hands together, a look of relief on his face. "Dude, you just made my day. I seriously don't think I could do sunrise."

Jenny threw Matt a half-smile. "Not even if Nancy Mulligan was there?"

Looking very solemn, Matt placed his hand over his heart. "Not even for Nancy Mulligan."

As the group laughed, Steve nodded to himself. The schedule worked out perfectly for them. The morning shoot gave the Decoders plenty of time to do some treasure hunting without anyone else around.

The camera operators moved into position and Jack excused himself to prepare for the shoot. The director called all the extras together and Steve saw Marisa give them a quick wave before the director instructed each of them where he wanted them to stand and what he wanted them to do. The three kids were kept together and told to stand in the middle of the street until the director yelled action and then they should begin walking. Then, once the two stunt doubles crashed through the saloon doors, the kids were to stop and watch the men get up and start fighting. That would be the end of this shot, and tomorrow the actors would continue the scene with the dialogue.

The trio got into position and waited. In fifteen minutes, the director finally yelled action and the scene began. The kids walked down the street and soon heard a small collision. Brian and Grant had crashed through the saloon doors and onto a cushioned pad placed on the ground for their landing. The kids stopped and watched the two stand up and take swings at each other.

"Cut!" The director yelled, then walked up to the stunt doubles and said something to them. "Again!" he yelled, and everyone returned to their original positions. Steve noticed one of the extras, a man in his mid-thirties, looking around nervously. Steve couldn't be positive, but he believed he was one of the men in the group they saw last night, possibly Sam or his friend.

They filmed the scene four more times, and throughout the filming, Steve kept his eyes on the strange man. Once the shoot was over, Steve saw him disappear behind one of the sets. Marisa waved at the kids again and began walking toward them.

"I'll be right back," Steve said to his friends before Marisa arrived. He glanced around to make sure no one saw him, then withdrew behind the set, hoping to find the mysterious man. He turned the corner just in time to see him head into a large shed the size of a small house. Knowing he couldn't follow him inside without being seen, Steve decided to wait him out. He didn't have to wait long. In less than a minute, the man walked out, looked both ways, and then left, closing the door behind him.

Steve waited a minute and then snuck up to the shed, opened the latch, and stepped inside. Windows all along the top allowed sunlight in so he could easily see. He took a quick survey as he walked around the room. The shed held all kinds of props from fake plants to paintings to weapons of all kinds, all made of plastic or plaster, but realistic nonetheless. He reached over and picked up one of the guns from a nearby table. It was incredibly light, much more so than a real one.

He continued his examination of the items, fascinated by all the different props, wondering if they would all be used at some point during the filming. Suddenly, he heard voices outside. Panicking, Steve glanced around and saw a closed wardrobe closet. He rushed over and yanked the door open. Several women's dresses hung within. Steve dove inside and crouched at the bottom, closing the wardrobe doors behind him, thankful for his small stature.

The sound of the shed door opening filled the air.

"Are you sure you lost it in here?" A man said. It sounded like the one called Sam they overheard talking the night before.

"Yeah," a second man said. "It was when Megan sent me in here to get the replacement gun for Grant. When I got back to the set, I noticed it had fallen out of my pocket." From their voices, Steve knew it was indeed the same two men.

Sam cursed. "If anyone finds it before we do, we won't be able to hide what we're doing here anymore."

Steve wished more than anything that he could push the door open and see who was talking, but he was afraid of making too much noise.

"Maybe we should just quit before anyone gets on to us," the second man said, his voice a bit shaky. "To tell you the truth, I'm not sure I even want to find the treasure any more, after what happened to Kevin. He was the reason we're even here."

"Kevin was…"

Crash! Something inside the wardrobe had fallen to the floor next to Steve.

A moment later, the wardrobe doors flew open and Steve found himself staring directly at the two men!

6 THE MINER'S PARTNER

Steve held his breath, unsure what to do.

"What are you doing here?" Sam demanded. He had short black hair underneath his cowboy hat and was dressed from head to toe in western duds, complete with a red bandana tied around his neck. The other man had sandy-blond hair and similar attire.

Steve thought furiously. The only thing he had going for him was that neither of the men knew him to be a detective. As far as they knew, he was just some dumb kid hired to be an extra for the movie. Steve decided to play the part.

He faked a look of fear. "Please don't tell on me," he said, making his voice quiver. "I…I know I'm not supposed to be in here, but I just wanted to see all the cool props." He climbed out of the closet. "They said I couldn't be here without an adult, but everyone is always so busy. I swear, I didn't touch anything. I promise. Oh, please don't tell Jack."

The sandy-haired man relaxed his face and shrugged. "It's all right, kid. We won't tell anyone."

Sam didn't look as convinced. He gave Steve a stern look. "Get out, and don't let us catch you in here again. Or else."

Steve nodded vigorously. "I won't. I promise." He rushed toward the shed doors. "Thanks a bunch!" He ran out and made his way over to Matt and Jenny, who stood talking with Marisa.

"There you are," Jenny said as he walked up. "We were wondering where you had run off to."

Steve smiled. "Sorry, I had to use the restroom."

Marisa glanced at her phone and sighed. "Well, looks like my short break is over. Jack wants me back at the saloon. See you kids later."

After she left, Jenny turned to Steve. "So, where'd you really go?"

Steve related everything that happened.

Matt whistled. "Dude, you're lucky those guys let you go. They could've knocked you out, tossed you in the back of a truck, driven you to the coast, and fed you to the sharks."

"Matt's exaggerations to the side," Jenny said, "it was kinda dangerous for you to follow someone alone. You should've taken one of us with you."

Steve nodded. "I know. To tell you the truth, I

didn't expect to wind up inside the shed, but once I saw him leave, I figured it was worth a shot."

"I wonder what fell out of his pocket," Jenny said.

"I don't know," Steve said. "But whatever it was, it had something to do with the treasure."

"And who's that Kevin dude, and what happened to him?" Matt asked. A loud cowbell rang through the air announcing dinner. Matt rubbed his hands together. "Greatest sound ever!"

"No doubt," Jenny agreed. "I am totally starving."

As the kids joined the crowd walking toward the mess tent, Steve glanced around hoping to get a look at Sam and his partner. If they had other accomplices, Steve would like to see them.

The smell of garlic and spaghetti sauce dominated the air, and the kids eagerly piled their plates with lasagna, spaghetti, salad, and breadsticks.

While walking through the crowded tables, they spotted Jack waving at them and made their way over to him. Steve took a seat next to Jack and the other two sat across from them.

Jack pointed to Matt's enormous pile of food and chuckled. "I see some things never change."

Matt pounded his fist into his chest. "I'm a growing boy. I need my strength."

"And at this rate," Jenny said as she popped

open her can of cola, "you'll be growing right out of your clothes."

Matt threw her an evil look and everyone laughed.

"How's the treasure hunt going?" Jack asked. "I know you had a scene this afternoon, but have you had a chance to work on it?"

Steve cut into a meatball on his plate. "Not really. After we went to the museum and spoke to the docent, we took pictures of the original note and purchased copies of the replica, but we haven't had time to study them yet."

"Not that it's gonna do us much good," Matt grumbled, "because apparently everybody on the planet bought a copy of that replica note."

"Are you aware of anyone who is seriously going after the treasure?" Steve asked Jack.

The older man shook his head. "I mean, everybody knows about it, and you're right, everyone has a copy of the note, but it's mostly just for fun. Nobody expects to actually find the treasure."

A gray-haired woman with a clipboard came up to the table. "Sorry to interrupt your dinner, Jack, but could you just give this one last look over?"

Jack put down his utensils and took the clipboard from her. He glanced over the front page then flipped quickly through the next few. "Everything looks good."

"Perfect." She looked relieved. "I'll see you tomorrow."

"Aren't you going to eat dinner?" Jack asked.

She shook her head. "Not now. There's too much to do. I'll grab something later."

As she scurried off, Jack pointed to her. "That is Mildred Johnson, our lead set designer. She's making sure we've got everything ready for tomorrow morning's shoot. It's a sunrise scene so everything has to be perfect and ready to go."

Wow," Jenny said. "That's sounds stressful. If like one thing goes wrong, you don't get another chance for twenty-four hours."

Jack nodded. "Exactly. The good thing is we only need one good shot of the sunrise, everything else we can add in later. But there is a chase scene that we want to film in the early morning hours, so we're filming that right after sunrise."

"Sounds like you're going to be pretty busy tomorrow," Steve said.

"Yep," Jack replied. "Most of the crew will be out there with us, and it's an early morning because we want to be ready for the sunrise, so we'll be setting up around four."

"Four in the morning?" Matt frowned. "Is that even a real time?"

"Yes, it is," Jack said, then a slow smile spread across his face. "So, breakfast is going to be at around three."

Matt choked on his drink and began coughing. Everyone laughed.

"Don't worry, Matt," Jack said. "I'll make sure they save you kids some food."

Matt gave a thumbs-up signal and took a swig of soda.

After piling his trash on his plate, Jack stood. "The early shoot also means an early night for most of the crew. If there's anything you need, let us know soon. It's going to get real quiet here pretty quick."

Steve nodded. "Thanks, Jack."

Once he left, Matt shook his head. "Three in the morning. That's crazy talk."

"That's perfect," Steve said, a sense of excitement growing inside him.

Matt gave him a wild look. "Now *you're* talking crazy. I love food and all, but getting up that early isn't normal."

"I'm not talking about getting up for food," Steve said. "I'm talking about tonight. You heard what Jack said. Most of the crew will be going to sleep early to prepare for the shoot. That means we can do some investigating without worrying about running into people."

Jenny wiped her mouth with her napkin then placed it on her plate. "Sounds good. But, where do we start?"

After thinking for a moment about different

possibilities, Steve made a decision. "The props shed."

Matt gave a short laugh. "You mean the place where the guy called Sam told you to never go back, or else?"

"Exactly," Steve said. "Whatever they were looking for had something to do with the treasure. It may still be in there."

Jenny frowned. "But what if they come back to look for it, too?"

"I thought of that," Steve answered. "We'll have to stake the place out first, then Jenny and I will search the shed while Matt acts as lookout."

"And what am I supposed to do if Sam and his partner show up?" Matt asked.

Steve shrugged. "Cause a distraction."

Jenny ruffled Matt's hair. "You're so good at that."

Matt groaned but agreed to the plan.

After dinner, the kids decided to hang out in Jenny's trailer and wait for the crew to turn in for the night. Matt plopped down on the loveseat. "I don't know about you guys, but I say we take a nap before our stakeout."

Steve sat next to him and pulled something out of his pocket. "I have a better idea."

Sitting on crossed legs on the edge of her bed, Jenny pointed to the piece of paper in Steve's hand. "Is that the replica?"

He nodded. "Since we've got some time to kill, I suggest we attempt to decipher it. Perhaps it can give us a clue as to what we should be looking for in the props shed."

"There goes nap time." Matt sighed.

Steve unfolded the note and cleared his throat. *"If you're reading this, then I be dead and the gold waits for you. Find the fountain and bathe in it to be clean before the journey. Then you can walk away and go to the land of flowers. Choose the rosiest and smell it hard. Then the real work begins. Squeeze like a lemon and then roll like dough. If you make it through the pipes, you're almost there. All you need is a shovel."* He looked up. "Any ideas?"

"Yeah," Matt said and held up his hand as if he were in school. "Let's take a nap."

Steve rolled his eyes. "I'm serious. What can we gather from this note?"

"It sounds like directions," Jenny said.

"You know what, dudes?" Matt scratched his chin. "It kinda reminds me of Elias Darby's note, the one from our first case."

"The same thought occurred to me," Steve said. "And Darby used his words to give us clues, so let's assume this is the same thing. The first sentence sounds like a challenge, like he's taunting us to find the gold."

Jenny pulled up the picture of the original note

on her cell and squinted. "Right. And, if this is, like, a dare, then the first thing we need to do is *find the fountain*. Whatever that means."

"Hey!" Matt sat up straight. "Maybe that's what that Sam dude and his buddy lost in the props room—a map to the fountain."

"I have an idea." Steve whipped out his cell phone and typed a quick text. A few moments later, the response came and he nodded. "Perfect."

"Mind telling us what's perfect?" Matt asked.

"I just asked Alysha to do a search for any nearby fountains or legends involving fountains in the area. She said she'd check it out and get back to us as soon as she could. In the meantime, let's keep going."

Jenny squinted at the screen. "*Find the fountain and bathe in it to be clean before the journey.* What could that mean?"

Matt laced his fingers behind his neck. "We need to take a bath before we start treasure hunting?"

"It sounds more like we need to climb inside the fountain in order to begin searching for the treasure." Steve bit his lip in thought. "Perhaps, wherever this fountain is, there's a hidden tunnel inside, one we need to climb inside to get to."

"Hey, yeah," Jenny said. "That kind of goes with the next part, *then you can walk away and go to the land of flowers.* Maybe, once we're through the tunnel, we'll end up in a meadow or something."

Stealing the replica note from Steve, Matt stared at it for a moment then handed it back. "I don't know. This all sounds like something out of *The Wizard of Oz*."

"What's the next part say?" Jenny asked, staring at her phone. "The pic on my cell is kinda blurry."

Steve held up the replica. "*Choose the rosiest and smell it hard.*"

Matt tossed up his hands in dramatic fashion. "Like I said, *The Wizard of Oz*."

Something about the passage did not make sense to Steve. "How would one pick the *rosiest* rose?"

"And why would we have to smell it?" Jenny added. "How would that help us find the treasure?"

Matt reached into the candy bowl on the nightstand and pulled out a Hershey's kiss. "How do we even know that this dude is legit? I mean, the man was dying when he wrote this. What if he wasn't in his right mind and we're sitting here like a bunch of losers trying to figure out a note left behind by a delusional old guy?"

Jenny teetered her head back and forth. "He's kinda got a point, crazy as that sounds. How do we know the miner even wanted anyone to find the gold? What if he left the note behind as a joke, never meaning for anyone to actually find his treasure?"

"Then why send for his friend?" Steve said. "Look at the words. Josiah wrote this note carefully, making sure each word was perfect, implying that it wasn't the ramblings of a crazy man, but a well thought out clue meant to give his friend the location of the treasure."

"Okay, okay, I give in. The note is legit." Matt tossed the chocolate wrapper toward the waste basket but missed. He got up to pick up his trash. "But what do all those things mean?"

"That's what we've got to figure out," Steve said with determination.

A knock on the door interrupted their conversation. Matt walked over and opened it. "Hey, Jack." He motioned for the man to enter the trailer.

"Hi, kids. I just wanted to let you know that most of the crew has already turned in for the night, and I'm heading to my trailer myself. But, if you need anything, Doug, the director's assistant, is on call." He pulled out a business card from his pocket and handed it to Matt. "Here's his cell number. Oh, and before I forget, I told the caterers to set aside three plates of food from breakfast for you guys so you don't have to worry about getting up early. The plates will be waiting for you down at the mess tent."

Matt clapped Jack on the shoulder before giving him a quick hug. "You are my hero, dude. Seriously."

Jack laughed. "No problem. You kids have a good night."

After saying good-night to Jack, Matt closed the door and walked back to the loveseat to sit down. "Okay, what's next?"

Steve's cell rang. He held the phone out as he answered. "Hey, Alysha. I've got you on speakerphone."

"Hey, guys. Hope I'm not interrupting anything."

"Not at all," Steve said. "We were just trying to decipher the miner's note. What's up?"

"I did some checking, like you asked, into the area around you. I couldn't find anything about a fountain or anything resembling a fountain that dates back to the days of the miner. There are some modern fountains in nearby towns, but all of them are recent, built within the past hundred years."

Steve scowled. "I was certain there would be some historical reference to a fountain."

"If there is," Alysha said, "I couldn't find it."

Steve shook his head even though Alysha couldn't see him. "No, I believe you. If you couldn't find anything, then it doesn't exist. The fountain the miner talked about must have been a clue that only his friend would recognize, something that only the two of them would get, but confuse other treasure seekers."

"Like us," Matt grumbled.

"I did find out some stuff about the miner's partner, Allen Jacobs, if you're interested," Alysha said.

Steve perked up and blurted out, "Absolutely!"

Alysha laughed. "Okay. It seems Allen Jacobs was not exactly the type of guy you'd choose to do business with. He was a small man wanted in several states for everything from bank robbing to murder. In fact, he avoided capture mainly because he was so small he could fit through tiny places that police couldn't follow him."

"Why would Josiah Carney even think of becoming partners with a guy like that?" Jenny asked. "I mean, how could you even trust him?"

Matt reached for another piece of chocolate. "Maybe he didn't know."

"Maybe that's why they had a falling out," Jenny said. "Carney found out the kind of guy Jacobs was, and wanted nothing to do with him."

Steve held up his hands in a slow-down motion. "Let's not get ahead of ourselves. We have no reason to think Carney and Jacobs didn't know each other beforehand. Remember, Carney was wanted by the law as well. It could be that they knew each other from before and then teamed up to look for gold. And, remember, people believed Carney left the note for Jacobs, so whatever their falling out was about, it must not have been that serious. What else did you find out about Jacobs?"

Alysha continued. "After fleeing from the law for several years, he joined with a group of Spanish pirates and raided ships in the Caribbean until their ship was sunk by a British naval vessel."

"What happened to him then?" Jenny asked.

"Nobody really knows. There's nothing else about him for almost ten years until he turned up in northern California and teamed up with Carney."

Steve chewed on his lower lip. "If Jacobs traveled with Spanish pirates, that could be the connection. Carney fled Virginia on a Spanish ship, perhaps that's when he met Jacobs."

"There's one more thing," Alysha said. "Allen Jacobs had a hook for his left hand."

"No way!" Matt said. "As in Captain Hook?"

Alysha laughed. "Yes, Matt, as in Captain Hook. During one of his last robberies, there was an accident and it severely injured his left hand, so he had the surgeon replace it with a hook."

"So creepy." Jenny shivered.

Lost in thought, Steve stared at the miner's note laying on the couch. If both Carney and Jacobs had been aboard Spanish pirate ships, then the miner's note could be written in some kind of pirate code.

"I've gotta go," Alysha's voice cut into his thoughts.

"Thanks for everything," Jenny said. "You're the best."

"Anytime. Let me know if you guys need more help."

Phone call over, Steve played with the cell in his hand, still lost in thought. The Decoders had encountered pirate's notes before, they usually involved booby traps and danger.

"Steve?" Matt said.

Steve shook his head to clear it, then looked back and forth between his friends

Matt's eyes narrowed. "You've got that crazy look in your eyes, the kind that usually ends with us getting into heaps of trouble."

"Wanna tell us what's going through your head?" Jenny said

Steve inhaled a deep breath and related his idea about a pirate's code to his friends.

Matt whistled. "So, if this note was written in a secret code, one that nobody but pirates who have been dead for two hundred years knew, then how are we supposed to figure it out?"

"Maybe there's something on the Internet about it?" Jenny suggested. "We could ask Alysha to look it up."

Steve nodded slowly. "That's probably a good idea."

"Why don't you look like you think that's a good idea?" Matt asked.

Steve teetered his head back and forth. "If the code is that easily accessible, then why hasn't anyone found the treasure yet?"

As he unwrapped another chocolate, Matt said, "Maybe nobody's figured out that the note is written in code."

"Or," Jenny added with a grin, "nobody's as smart as we are."

Steve beamed at the comment. As crazy as that sounded, it was possibly true. Not that they were so incredibly smart, but they had Alysha, and chances were, most treasure seekers didn't look that deeply into the miner's past. His smile faded. Except for Sam and his cohort. Something told Steve those two would be the detectives' major rivals. He set his jaw. "Who's ready to go out and do some investigating?"

7 MUDDY FOOTPRINTS

Steve looked back and forth between his two friends.

Jenny jumped up. "I'm ready!"

Matt stood as well, although not quite as dramatically as Jenny, and nodded. "Me, too."

As the trio headed toward the door, Steve put the compass in his pocket, just in case. Most likely they wouldn't be going out into the desert at night, even Steve knew how dangerous that could be, but they'd been in situations before where they'd started out in one place, and ended up in the middle of the desert. Better to be prepared for anything.

After taking a quick peek outside and seeing no one in sight, they left the trailer and walked silently toward the set.

"It is seriously spooky out here right now," Jenny whispered, "like, horror movie spooky."

"Dudes, can we not talk about horror movies right now?" Matt said.

Steve made no comment, but couldn't help but agree. Even though they'd been all over this area throughout the day, the silence of night gave the place an eerie vibe. "Let's head toward the prop shed," he said.

The detectives walked as quietly as they could while constantly looking around to be sure no one saw them. They reached the shed without seeing any movement.

Steve pulled his partners in close and spoke in a low voice. "Okay, Matt. Here's where we split up. You keep your eyes open for Sam and his partner, or anyone else for that matter. We don't want anyone to think we're snooping around without permission."

"Copy that," Matt said.

Jenny frowned. "Did you just seriously say *copy that?*"

A smile spread across his face. "Yep. Just trying to get into…" he paused, put his hands on his hips, and rocked his head back and forth "the zone."

Jenny groaned. "Matt, please tell me you're not watching reruns of *Police Puppies on the Go*."

"I just found my old DVD." Matt's grin grew wider. "Those shows were the best."

Steve looked at Jenny curiously.

Jenny rolled her eyes. "We used to watch this

show back in like first grade about these five puppies who turned into superheroes whenever their owners were in danger. Matt would crawl around on the floor, then jump up and scream that he was in *the zone*. It was so ridiculous."

"My mom thought it was cute," Matt said.

"She was just being nice," Jenny retorted. "She's a good mom."

Steve chuckled, picturing a little Matt crawling around like a superhero puppy. "Okay, let's get back to business. If you see anyone coming, try and distract them so we can get out."

"How should I do that?" Matt asked as Steve carefully unlatched the shed door.

"Maybe you could start barking," Jenny said. "That always worked for Police Puppies."

"Just keep them occupied in conversation long enough for us to get out." Steve pushed the door open and walked into the shed, followed closely by Jenny, who closed the door behind her.

The two kids turned on the flashlight apps on their cells. As he moved his light around, Steve noticed that most of the props he had seen earlier were still in the same place. Sam and his cohort did not seem to have disturbed anything.

"What are we looking for?" Jenny asked, her voice barely above a whisper.

"I'm not sure. Anything that doesn't belong here and is small enough to fit in a man's pocket."

The kids split up. Steve headed to the right, toward the weapons. Sam's partner said he had been sent there to get a replacement gun, so perhaps he lost whatever it was somewhere around the fake guns.

He reached the weapons table and knelt on the floor, scanning the area with his light. Nothing. He crawled around, thinking perhaps the missing item had rolled away somewhere. Still finding nothing, he stood and scanned the table itself, carefully examining each row of weapons. Multiple knives sat lined up in two neat rows. Steve grabbed one and followed the blade with his finger, then bent it back. Rubber. He put it down and touched a couple other knives to see if they were also made of rubber.

Next, he turned his attention to the rows of firearms. There were multiple different types of guns, from revolvers to shotguns. He picked up one of the small handguns and felt the lightness in his hand. It was made of plastic, not metal. Steve guessed them to be cheaper to buy than metal and looked just as real. He picked up each gun to look underneath, but found nothing out of the ordinary. When he was half-way through, Jenny touched his shoulder.

"Hey, Steve," she said. "What do you make of this?" She held up a small piece of paper rolled like a mini scroll.

Steve put down his cell and took the paper from

Jenny's hand, then unrolled it. He frowned. "It's just a bunch of numbers."

Looking over his shoulder at the paper, Jenny commented, "Looks like nothing."

Steve had a strange feeling that the numbers were important, but he had no idea why. After staring at them for a few more seconds, he rolled the paper back up and placed it in his pocket. "Let's finish our investigation."

At that moment, the shed door opened and Matt poked his head inside. "How's it going in here?"

"Slow." Steve sighed. "What's happening outside?"

"Total deadsville, dude."

Steve motioned for Matt to come inside. "Why don't you help us look around? It'll go faster and we can get out of here sooner."

"Sounds good." Matt turned on his flashlight app.

As Steve resumed his search of the weapons table, he heard shuffling behind him.

"Hey, guys," Matt said. "What do you think?"

Steve turned around to see Matt wearing an enormous Mexican sombrero. Steve couldn't help but laugh. The boy looked ridiculous.

Matt grinned and held up two fingers. "I'll take dos tacos, dos enchiladas, and mucho guacamole."

Jenny's face cringed. "That may be the worst Spanish accent I've ever heard."

Matt pounded his chest. "Yo es Matt and yo tener hambre."

Chuckling, Steve shook his head. "First of all, it would be yo *soy* Matt and yo *tengo* hambre. And second, please take that hat off before you offend the entire Hispanic culture."

Matt laughed and put the sombrero next to several cowboy hats on a rack. "Dude, my Spanish is way improving."

Jenny cleared her throat and smiled. "We'll have to ask Rosa next time she's in town."

Even the darkness of the shed couldn't hide Matt's face turning red. Rosa was a client the three detectives helped a few weeks ago, and Matt clearly had a huge crush on her, even if he refused to admit it.

Steve knew he better intervene before Jenny began teasing Matt mercilessly. "Let's finish this and get out of here. We still have other stuff to do."

The three searched the shed in silence, then after fifteen minutes decided to abandon their efforts.

After peeking out to make sure no one was in sight, Steve motioned for his friends to follow him out and the three kids headed back toward their trailer.

"So, now what?" Jenny asked.

"Think there's any snacks at the mess tent?" Matt asked.

"Geez, Matt." Jenny gave him a slight push. "Do you ever think about anything besides—"

"What are you kids doing out here?" A loud voice interrupted.

The kids whirled around to see Peggy Ayers, the camera gal, holding up a flashlight as she walked up to them.

Steve thought fast. "Hi, Peggy," he said in a casual voice. "We were bored, and since everyone's asleep, we figured we'd just take a good look at all the sets. We don't get a lot of time to do that during the day because everybody's always all over the place."

"We were just about to head over to the mess tent and see if there's any snacks around," Matt added. "Do you know if they keep the chips out at night?"

Steve studied the woman. Her expression appeared concerned, but he had no idea why.

"Well, you shouldn't be out here this late." She glanced around. "You need to head back to your trailer."

Steve frowned. The woman looked nervous. Who, or what, was she worried about?

"So, no snacks?" Matt said, his voice clearly disappointed. Steve guessed it was probably not an act.

"No," she said, still looking around. "They don't keep any of the food out at night. Now, you should get back to your trailers and stay there until morning."

The kids agreed and walked back to Jenny's trailer. Once inside with the door closed, Jenny whirled around. "Okay, that was weird, right?"

With one big leap, Matt jumped up onto the couch. "Totally. Why don't they have snacks out overnight? I mean, what if someone gets a snack attack at like midnight and then passes out from lack of food?"

Jenny threw a pillow at him.

Steve sat on the couch next to Matt and crossed his arms. "Something was definitely weird about this. Did you notice her shoes?"

Matt climbed down to take a seat. "Seriously?"

"What about her shoes?" Jenny asked as she sat on the edge of the bed.

"They were covered in mud. Fresh mud. The dirt out here is as dry as, well, dirt. Why would she have fresh mud on her shoes? Where did it come from?"

Reaching for a piece of chocolate, Matt said, "Maybe she's getting something ready for the morning shoot."

Steve shook his head. "Jack said they were done setting up, so there would be no reason for her to be out this late."

"So then, what do you think she was doing?" Jenny asked.

"Good question," Steve said. "And did you notice her glancing around?"

Matt held up his finger. "I actually did catch that. I figured she was just checking if anyone else was out there. But, now that you mention it, she was acting kinda paranoid."

Steve nodded. "As if she was nervous that someone would see us."

"But, why?" Jenny asked.

Steve set his jaw. "I intend to find out." He stood.

"Hold up," Matt said. "She told us we weren't supposed to be out. Don't you think she'd get mad if she saw us snooping around? And what if we run into whoever she didn't want to see us?"

"We'll just have to be careful." Steve headed for the door.

The three detectives walked quietly toward the last spot they had seen the camera operator. No movement anywhere.

"Now what?" Matt asked.

Steve thought for a moment. If she had mud on her boots, then she had to be somewhere outside the set, somewhere in the desert. "Let's head toward the trail."

"Stop, dude." Matt grabbed Steve's arm and pulled him back. "I have to draw the line here. That's seriously dangerous. There's wolves and snakes out there. For real."

Steve patted Matt's arm. "Don't worry, we're not going *on* the trail. Not now. I just want to see if that's where Peggy came from. There'd be muddy footprints leading back and we need to check now before they dry up." Noticing Matt's face still looked concerned, he continued. "And, if we do see the footprints, then tomorrow morning, while everyone, including Peggy, is working on the shoot, we can check out where the footprints lead."

Matt's face relaxed and he released Steve's arm. "Okay, that makes sense."

As the three friends made their way toward the dirt path, Steve turned on his flashlight app but told the others to keep theirs off. Too much light could draw attention. They approached the path and Steve shown his light down.

Just as he suspected—muddy footprints.

"You were right," Jenny said.

"What the heck was she doing out there in the middle of the night?" Matt asked. "And where did the mud even come from? There's no water out here."

"I don't know," Steve said. "But, I intend to find out tomorrow."

Suddenly, Steve felt a sharp pain on the back of his head and everything went dark.

8 A BAD SITUATION

Steve opened his eyes slowly. The back of his head throbbed. He winced and tried to raise his arm to touch it, but couldn't. Panic gripped him. Wide awake now, he struggled to move his arms and noticed his hands had been tied behind his back. He inhaled a deep breath and stopped squirming to analyze the situation.

He was sitting on dirt with his legs in front of him. His hands were tied behind his back, and a rope wound tightly around his chest, tying him to a tree. His head throbbed.

"Dude, you okay?"

Steve glanced around and saw Matt, in the same tied-up situation, at a tree to his left. Steve nodded. "Yes, my head just hurts. Where's Jenny?"

"I'm here," Jenny said, tied similarly to his right.

"What happened?" Matt asked. "Last thing I remember, we were looking at the footprints, and then, bam! Something hit me in the back of the head."

Steve nodded. "That's exactly what happened to me."

"Not me," Jenny said. "We were checking out the muddy prints, and then someone grabbed me from behind and put a wet cloth over my face. It smelled funny. Next thing I know, I wake up here."

"Sounds like you were drugged," Steve said.

Matt grunted. "Glad they didn't whack *you* on the head. I'd have to crack some skulls."

"Yeah," Jenny said, "those guys were real gentlemen."

"If they were even *guys*," Steve said.

Matt gulped. "You think they were gh…ghosts?"

"No, Matt," Steve said, slightly annoyed. "I'm saying perhaps they weren't *men* that attacked us. We were out there investigating Peggy's footprints, remember?"

"Hey, that's right," Jenny said. "It could have been women."

Matt grunted. "Well, the dudette that whacked me must have a mean left hook. My head's killing me."

The throbbing of Steve's own head seemed to mirror his friend's complaint. "Let's think about this logically. We were all attacked simultaneously, therefore there had to be three of them."

"Right," Jenny said.

"Matt and I were both hit hard on the head," Steve continues, "which would be more likely done by men. My guess would be Sam and his accomplice. But Jenny was drugged, most likely chloroform. It's possible her assailant was female."

"Like Peggy," Jenny said.

"Exactly."

Matt whistled. "So, Peggy is in on it with those two creeps?"

"Possibly," Steve said. "We really have no proof of any of this because none of us saw anything. In reality, it could've been anyone."

"Including the miner's ghost," Matt added.

Steve rolled his eyes. "Okay, anyone but *that*."

"Um, guys," Matt said in a voice barely above a whisper.

"Steve's right, Matt," Jenny said. "I'm pretty sure the person who grabbed me was not a ghost."

"Dudes, be quiet." Matt was stern. "Listen."

The three kids became silent.

Jenny's whisper pierced the darkness. "Is…is that a rattlesnake?"

Steve did not respond but focused his attention on the sound. It was indeed a rattlesnake and close by, no more than fifteen feet judging by the sound of it.

Knowing he had to act fast before his friends put themselves in danger, Steve said in a calm voice, "Whatever you do, don't make any movement. Rattlesnakes are deaf, but they can sense vibrations, so the more you move, the more aware of you he'll become. And, if he perceives you as a threat…"

They sat in complete stillness, yet the rattling continued.

"Um, Steve," Jenny murmured, "we're not making any moves, why is he still rattling?"

Steve bit his lip, hoping his ears deceived him. They didn't. "Because," he whispered back, "something else is scaring him."

A low growling came from behind them.

"Whatever you do, don't move." Steve felt his heart racing inside his chest.

Seconds later, another growl came from his right and another from his left. A pack of wolves had detected them, and he and his friends were tied down to trees.

Steve thought furiously, but could think of no way out of this situation. Wolves had phenomenal hearing and could hear sounds up to six miles away, so they undoubtedly had heard the Decoders talking, and, to make matters worse, wolves had superior eyesight enabling them to see at night. And, they usually hunted in packs of no less than six and could run around thirty miles an hour. Even if the kids could miraculously get out of their ropes and run, they'd be outpaced and outnumbered.

Jenny whimpered and Steve could tell she was crying. They needed a miracle.

Suddenly, a gunshot rang through the air. The shooter was close. The growling stopped. Steve looked around wildly. A series of gunshots rang, and Steve caught quick images of light with each shot fired and waves of smoke coming from the gun. Judging by the direction the smoke drifted and the sparks flying up, Steve could tell that the shooter had aimed his gun up into the air and not at the wolves themselves.

The sound of scurrying paws filled the air and Steve knew the animals had withdrawn. Even the rattlesnake was gone. The mystery shooter had saved their lives.

"Thank you!" Steve called out.

No response.

"We owe you our lives," he continued. "Who are you?"

No response.

Faintly, the detective heard footsteps retreating. Whoever their rescuer was, he or she did not want to be seen. Steve frowned. Who could it be?

"That was close," Matt said, relief apparent in his voice. "I thought we were toast. And, by toast I mean a wolf-sized steak with a side of mashed potatoes."

Jenny laughed. also sounding relieved. "You know that didn't make any sense, right?"

"We need to get out of here." Steve began wrestling with the rope binding his hands. "Those wolves could come back."

"OMG, I just remembered," Jenny said. "I've got my pocket knife in my back pocket. I'm pretty sure I can get to it."

"Good," Steve said. "because mine's in my front pocket and impossible to get to."

"Mine, too," Matt said.

The boys waited while Jenny pulled out her knife and began working on her ropes. A few moments later, she had her hands free and then used the knife to cut the rope binding her to the tree.

After several minutes, she had freed both boys and the three kids pulled out their cell phones and turned on the flashlights.

"Where do you guys think we are?" Jenny asked as she scanned the area.

Steve did not respond. He had no idea where the kidnappers had brought them. They were surrounded by trees and could easily be miles away from the movie set. And, with no weapons to fight off the wolves, they could be in serious danger.

Matt looked up at the sky and pointed at the stars. "Okay, so that way's north. What direction do you think we need to go?"

Steve bit his lip, trying to come up with a plan.

"Let's head to the spot where the shooter stood. Hopefully, he or she followed a trail to get here, one we can follow to get…somewhere."

Matt agreed. "Sounds better than just wandering around aimlessly in the desert in the middle of the night."

Keeping close together, they made their way to the spot where they had seen the gun sparks and smoke. As they approached, Steve shone his light on the dirt and began searching for a path.

"Hey, guys," Jenny said, "over here. I found footprints."

The boys walked over and looked at the ground.

"Bummer, dudes," Matt said. "There's no trail."

"No," Steve said, "but our best shot at finding a way out of here is to follow those footprints."

"It's gonna be slow going," Jenny said. "They're like scattered because there's no path."

Afraid the footprints would disappear like they had earlier, Steve knew they had to act quickly. "Let's get going."

They stepped carefully, making sure to search all around, before moving, to not lose the trail.

After nearly half an hour, Jenny stopped and pointed. "Hey, check it out! A path!"

The footprints led to a small dirt trail and then continued to a path.

"Hold up, guys," Matt said. "Are we sure we want to follow the path in the same direction as the shooter? I mean, the dude has a gun. Maybe we should go the other way."

"He may have a gun, but he saved our lives," Steve pointed out. "If he wanted to harm us, he could've let the wolves do the job for him."

"That's true," Matt conceded.

Steve stepped onto the trail. "Come on."

As the kids began their trek on the path, Jenny asked, "Who do you think the shooter was, anyway?"

"I've been thinking about that since he saved us," Steve said.

"If it's even a *he*," Jenny said. "It could be a *she*."

Steve shook his head. "The footprints are clearly a man's."

"Any idea who?" Matt asked. "Because I'd really like to give him a shout out."

"I think it's one of our kidnappers," Steve said.

"Wait. Seriously?" Matt said. "You think the dude kidnapped us, tied us to a tree to be wolf food, and then came back out here to save us? That's crazy talk."

"I'm gonna have to agree with Matt on this one," Jenny said. "That doesn't make any sense."

"I know it sounds crazy," Steve admitted, "but it's the only logical explanation. Who else would know we were out there? My thought is that one of the kidnappers didn't agree with his partners about leaving us out there, and then came back, alone, to help us."

"You know," Matt said, "there is one other possibility. There's someone else who might have been out in the desert and who might have seen us."

Steve looked at Matt, surprised. "Who?"

Matt paused. "The miner."

Steve rolled his eyes. "Matt—"

"It wasn't the miner," Jenny interrupted.

"Thank you," Steve said.

"The footprints were off," Jenny continued. "The miner has way small footsteps, remember?"

"Oh, yeah." Matt nodded. "I forgot."

Steve stared at the girl. "Why do you encourage him?"

"It's just so fun!" Jenny laughed.

Matt pointed back and forth between his friends. "You guys watch. One day, we're going to meet a real ghost and then you're gonna be sorry you didn't listen to me."

"Oh," Jenny said, "I'm already sorry I listen to you." The three friends burst out laughing.

As they continued following the trail in silence. Steve attempted to wrap his head around who the kidnappers could've been. The logical choice would be Sam and his partner, and most likely Peggy. But what would Peggy be doing partnering up with two clearly unscrupulous men, and what would the three of them be doing out in the middle of the night? If they were searching for the treasure, it would be near impossible to see anything in the dark, so then what were they doing?

And who came back to rescue them? It certainly wasn't Peggy's footprints they had found, but then whose? Sam's partner did seem more timid; perhaps he felt bad and came back to help.

"Hey, guys!" Matt's voice cut into Steve's thoughts. "Check it out. I think I see lights up ahead."

It soon became clear that there were indeed lights in the distance ahead of them.

"They look like street lights," Jenny said.

Matt squinted. "I think you're right. Come on." He picked up the pace with the others right behind him.

Within a few minutes, they were close enough to make out buildings in the distance.

"I recognize that place," Matt said, sounding relieved. "It's the town by the movie set. See?" He pointed. "There's the museum up on the left."

"You're right." Jenny clapped. "That means we're close to home."

Steve glanced at the time on his cell phone. "We need to hurry."

"Why?" Jenny asked, as she attempted to match his steps.

"Because it's almost two o'clock," he replied. "The movie crew will be getting up soon, and I don't think they would be happy about three kids running around at this hour of the night unsupervised."

Jenny nodded. "That makes sense."

"Hey," Matt chimed in, "do you think they've started cooking breakfast yet?"

"It doesn't matter," Steve said. "We're not showing up for breakfast. We need to get some sleep so we can get up early and do some exploring while the crew is filming."

Matt groaned. "Like how early, exactly?"

Knowing his friend's reaction ahead of time, Steve hesitated. "Six."

"In the morning?" Matt said. "That's in like four hours."

Steve sighed. "I know, but they're filming a sunrise scene and the sun rises at five forty-five. Getting up at six will give us time to go get the breakfast Jack promised and then head out to investigate."

In dramatic fashion, Matt groaned again, but said nothing. By three o'clock, the kids had made it to their trailers, agreeing to meet at six for breakfast.

As Steve prepared for bed, his thoughts returned to the mysterious shooter. The man had clearly saved the trio's lives. But who could it be? If he was Sam's accomplice, why risk angering Sam by freeing the kids. If it wasn't the accomplice, then who was it and what were they doing out there in the middle of the night? Sighing, Steve pulled the covers up. One thing was for sure, the treasure hunt had become far more dangerous than he had anticipated.

9 THE FOUNTAIN

At 6:15, the trio arrived at the mess tent. A caterer waved them over and handed them each a plate of breakfast foods. Steve thanked the man and led his friends to a table.

Matt yawned as he sat down. They were alone in the tent. "I am seriously so tired. And hungry."

After setting down her plate, Jenny stretched her arms overhead. "Me, too. The tired part, not so much the hungry part."

Matt pointed to her food. "Let me know if you need help finishing any of that off."

As he unrolled the plastic silverware from the napkin, Steve commented, "We should all try to eat as much as possible. We'll most likely be gone all morning, and we'll need our strength."

"No problem there." Matt stuffed a mound of hash browns into his mouth.

"So, what's the plan?" Jenny asked as she spread some strawberry jelly on her toast.

Steve cut into the ham slice on his plate. "We head over to where we saw Peggy's muddy footprints last night. They're probably dry, but we can still try to follow them. I don't know why or how, but I believe she is mixed up with Sam and his cohort, and whatever the three of them are up to, it's no good."

Matt poured ketchup on the side of his plate. "I had an idea last night as I was falling asleep."

"Wow," Jenny said, "that must have taken you by surprise."

"Ha ha." Matt threw her an evil look. "I'm serious."

Jenny laughed. "Okay, I'm just kidding. What's up?"

"I was thinking about Peggy's muddy footprints." He shook his carton of chocolate milk. "Remember the beginning of the miner's note? It said something about looking for a fountain. What if Peggy found the fountain?"

Fork half-way to his mouth, Steve froze. After a moment, he set down the fork and reached for his phone. "Matt, you are brilliant."

"I know." Matt grinned widely. "I got mad skills."

Jenny rolled her eyes. "Ugh. Why can't you just take a compliment like a normal person?"

Steve scrolled through the pictures on his camera roll. "This is it. *Find the fountain and bathe in it to be clean before the journey.*" He looked up. "I think Matt's right. If Peggy located the fountain, then it would explain her wet shoes last night."

"Which means that she's one step closer to finding that treasure than we are," Jenny said.

Steve set his jaw. "Not for long. They'll be shooting all morning. Come on. Let's hurry so we can get out there."

Once they finished eating and disposed of their trash, the kids each grabbed a bottle of water and put it into their mystery backpacks, then left for their investigation.

"Over here," Steve said as they reached the footprints. "Like we figured, the prints are dry, but they're still visible."

"Then let's see where they go," Jenny said, and the trio set off into the desert.

They walked for almost fifteen minutes before Steve stopped them.

"What's up?" Matt asked.

Steve pointed to the ground. "The footprints veer off the trail here."

"Then that's where we need to go," Jenny said and stepped over a small bush heading the direction of the footprints.

"Hold on," Steve said, gently pulling Jenny's arm. "We need to be smart about this."

"Everyone's out on the shoot," Jenny said. "We should be good."

Steve shook his head. "That's not what I mean. The last time we followed footprints out here, they mysteriously disappeared and we almost got lost. We need to leave a trail, one that we can follow in case we get lost or Peggy's footprints disappear."

Matt nodded. "Good thinking." He frowned. "But, how?"

"I came prepared." Steve took off his small backpack and opened it, pulling out a roll of masking tape.

"We're going to put tape down on the ground?" Matt asked. "Not to burst your bubble, dude, but that roll has only got about fifty yards of tape, and I'm pretty sure we're gonna be going further than that."

"I'm not going to lay it on the ground. Steve ripped off a small piece of tape. "I'm going to tie a piece of it to a bush every twenty or thirty feet, so we can follow them on the way back."

Matt clapped Steve on the shoulder. "Dude, you're one smart kid."

"I know." Steve said, grinning.

Jenny rolled her eyes. "Okay, wow. Do you guys like practice feeding each other's egos?"

Matt and Steve laughed and the three continued their trek, with Steve stopping every so often to tie a piece of masking tape to a bush.

After about a half hour, the footprints stopped. Steve bent down and touched the ground. "The dirt feels damp. There must be an underground spring or water source of some kind."

Matt looked around and scratched his chin. "Nothing around here looks like a fountain."

"I know." Steve surveyed the area. "But this is where Peggy's footprints end. And the ground is wet. Spread out. Let's look for clues."

The trio split up, each searching a different area. Steve concentrated on the ground near the footprints. There would be no logical reason for Peggy to be out here in the middle of the night unless she was looking for the treasure. The odd thing was that only *her* footprints were around. No others. Why would she be here alone if she had partnered with Sam and his accomplice?

"Hey, guys," Matt's voice cut into his thoughts. "Over here."

Steve and Jenny joined Matt, who pointed down. "It looks like a ravine. There's no path, but I think I could slide down pretty easily. Think I should check it out?"

Steve studied the gorge with interest. Although not large in area, the ravine did have a significant number of plants and shrubs dotting it, some of which most certainly required water for survival. He whirled around and clapped Matt on the shoulder. "Matt! I think you found it!"

"Found what?" Matt looked confused. "The ravine?"

"The fountain!" Steve tried to control his excitement and pointed down. "Look at all the plants. Well-watered plants. There must be an underground water source that is feeding them all. And judging by the rocks layered in the ravine, I would say that this area used to hold water."

"Hold water?" Jenny repeated. "So, a hundred and fifty years ago, this might've looked like a big pool."

"Or," Steve said triumphantly, "a fountain. Come on. According to the miner, we've got to bathe in it before we can start the journey."

As he began his descent, Steve slid on some loose rocks and lost his balance.

Matt caught him before he fell. "Dude, better let me lead."

Steve caught his breath and agreed, knowing Matt to be much better at outdoor activities than himself.

After scanning the area, Matt chose the route he believed to be the safest. The steep hill presented challenges, and several times the trio had to sit on the ground and slide to keep from tumbling down. Finally, after a few bruises and scratches, the detectives made it to the bottom.

Jenny wiped some dirt off her jeans. "Okay, now what?"

Steve pulled out his cell phone and scrolled to the miner's note. *"Find the fountain and bathe in it to be clean before the journey. Then you can walk away and go to the land of flowers."* He looked up. "What do you guys think?"

Jenny's eyebrows knit together. "If there was water here back in the miner's time, then, technically, we'd be bathing in the fountain right now."

"So now we're supposed to go to the land of flowers," Matt said. "Whatever that means."

Steve bit his lip as he surveyed the area. A number of shrubs had flowers, but they wouldn't have been around during the time of the miner. This would've all been underwater. "We need to spread out and look for something that has to do with flowers. And, remember, it needs to be over a hundred and fifty years old, so don't look for anything living."

"No real flowers," Matt said. "Got it."

The three friends split up again, each heading in a different direction.

As Steve scanned the area, something felt off. If this area had been underwater during the miner's time, then how could he expect them to find anything? He pushed a bit of sweat up into his slight afro, then glanced at his watch. It was only seven-thirty but the temperature had already begun to climb. He stopped and took a drink from his bottled water. As he returned it to his backpack, he continued his contemplation.

If the water in the ravine was clear, then one bathing in it could possibly see to the bottom. He frowned. But that seemed unlikely. The dirt in the area was reddish, thus making it probable that the water would have been murky. So, what did Josiah want them to look for?

He stumbled around for another few minutes until something caught his eye. There, in the hill ahead of him, lay a path leading up out of the ravine. At the top stood a large collection of boulders, meaning that the path would've been impossible to detect from above. "Matt! Jenny! Over here!"

"What's up?" Jenny asked as she and Matt approached.

Steve pointed, trying to control his enthusiasm. "I think I found it! The way to the land of flowers."

Matt glanced at the path and shrugged. "It's a path, I'll give you that. But I thought we were looking for the land of flowers down here."

"That's just it," Steve said, his excitement mounting. "I think we had it wrong. The note said to bathe in the fountain and then walk away to the land of flowers. My theory is that if this ravine had been filled with water, then only someone bathing in it could see this path."

Matt grumbled. "I wish we had seen the path

before we slid down the ravine on our butts. I'm gonna have some serious bruises from that."

"No doubt," Jenny agreed. "But, Steve. Matt brings up a good point—shockingly enough—"

"Ha, ha," Matt interjected.

"What I mean is," Jenny continued, "if the path just leads out of here, why not just start the journey at the top? Why would he tell us to get into the fountain?"

"Because," Steve answered, "the path isn't visible from the top, only from down here. Look." He pointed up. "See the boulders? If we were up there, we'd never see the path. Josiah needed his partner to be at the top of this path to begin the journey, and the only way he could be sure Jacobs would find the path was to make sure he was in the fountain to start off with."

Jenny nodded her head slowly. "So then, if we want to go to the land of the flowers, then we've got to climb the path."

"Exactly!" Steve said triumphantly.

"All right, then, dudes." Matt took a few steps. "Let's get going. It's starting to get hot out here."

The others agreed and fell in line behind Matt. As they neared the top, the path itself disappeared and the trio had to carefully maneuver their way around the large rocks.

"Careful climbing that last one," Matt said once he reached the top. "It's a little loose."

"Whoa," Jenny said as the rock moved under her weight. "You weren't kidding. Be careful, Steve."

Steve grunted as he lifted his leg to get over the large stone. Suddenly, the rock began to move under him. In a split second, Steve realized the boulder had come loose from the mountain and was starting to tumble down the hill, taking Steve with it!

10 THE LAND OF FLOWERS

Panicked, Steve made a last-ditch effort to jump.

"Gotcha!" Matt said as he grabbed Steve's arm, preventing the boy from taking a massive tumble.

Steve watched the large rock roll down the hill, knocking other rocks loose and creating a massive cloud of dust.

"Thanks," Steve said as his friend helped him up.

"That was close," Jenny said. "Are you okay?"

Ignoring Jenny, Steve watched the massive dust cloud move up toward the sky. "That is not good."

"Could be worse," Matt said. "You could have joined the giant dust cloud in the sky." He grinned. "Get it? Cloud in the sky?"

Jenny groaned. "Seriously, Matt, I think the sun is like totally getting to you."

"What I meant," Steve interrupted, "is that now

everyone will see the dust cloud and know that we're out here and where we are."

Matt's smile disappeared. "And by everyone you mean the dudes who tied us up and left us for wolf food."

Steve nodded. "Exactly."

As she let down her hair to re-tie it in a ponytail, Jenny said, "Then we've got to hurry up and find the land of flowers."

Steve examined the area. Clearly, this was where the miner wanted his friend to be to begin his search for the treasure. "Come on," he said and began walking. "The miner's note said to *walk away*, so let's head out. Keep your eyes peeled for anything that resembles flowers."

They continued their trek in silence. Steve wiped more sweat off his brow. It was, by far, the hottest day so far and they had each only brought one bottle of water with them. The dust cloud worried him, too. Even though Peggy was busy all morning with the shoot, Sam and his cohort could be free and searching for the treasure. Or them.

Scanning the ground as he walked, Steve did his best to avoid the large number of loose rocks all around. What could the miner have meant by the land of flowers? If he meant literal flowers, then he must've assumed that his friend would be coming here to search for the treasure immediately. But that didn't seem likely. The two friends had a falling out. The miner couldn't have known when his friend would be coming to search for the treasure. It would make more sense for him to leave clues that would be around for a while. Steve frowned. But would the clues still be around a hundred and fifty years later?

Suddenly, he tripped over a large stone and crashed down on the ground. Wincing, he sat up and rubbed his left knee. "That will definitely leave a bruise." He mumbled to himself.

He stood and wiped the dust off his pants and shirt, then looked at the stone that had caused him to fall. It was the size of a man's fist and round, almost perfectly round, with a flat top. Steve picked it up and examined it closely. Etched very faintly into the stone were scratches. He licked his finger and rubbed the dust off the stone to study it in greater detail.

The scratches were man-made, he was sure of it. He extended his arm and stared at the stone from a distance.

"Matt! Jenny!" He called out. "Over here."

Once the two friends joined him, Steve showed them the stone. "Look at this."

Matt stared at it and then up at Steve. "It's a rock."

"I know it's a rock," Steve said impatiently, "but look at the etchings someone carved into it."

Jenny grabbed the stone out of Steve's hand.

After a few seconds, she shrieked. "OMG, it's a flower!"

"Let me see that." Matt reached over and took it from her. After a few seconds, he nodded and handed it to Steve. "Yep. That's definitely a flower. Where'd you find it?"

"Over here." Steve pointed to the ground behind him. "I tripped over it."

Jenny looked around. "That means there might be more of them around."

"That's what I'm thinking," Steve said. "The only problem is they're all covered in dirt. They might be hard to find."

Matt took a swig of water from his bottle. "Let's get to it then."

The trio spread out to search for more stones. After a half hour, they had discovered twenty rocks with the flower etchings, and used twigs to mark the locations to not remove the stones from their places.

"I have a question," Matt said as he placed a twig near his latest find. "What happens once we find all the flowers?"

Steve pulled out his cell, read the miner's note, then cleared his throat. "We need to choose the rosiest and smell it hard."

"How do we know which one is the rosiest?" Matt asked.

Steve was about to answer that he had no idea when Jenny interrupted.

"Hey, guys. Over here." She waved them over. "Houston, I think we have a problem." She squatted down and pointed to a softball-sized rock. "See this rock? It has the etchings on it, too. But it was face down. I wouldn't have even noticed it, but I was marking the one a couple feet away and just out of curiosity, I picked it up."

"But if some of the rocks are face down," Matt said, "then how are we supposed to find them all? There could be hundreds of them out here."

Steve frowned and bit his lip. The miner wouldn't have made it this difficult for his friend. He rubbed his temples and thought furiously. They were missing something.

"And not to make things worse," Matt said as he unscrewed the top of his water bottle, "but I'm almost out of water and it's getting seriously hot out here."

Steve sighed and wiped more sweat off his forehead. "Let's head back to the set. You're right, it's getting too hot to be out here much longer, and we've got to take a closer look at the miner's note. Something in there must give us a clue as to what we're supposed to do."

The walk back toward the movie set was slow, as a late morning breeze had erased Peggy's footprints and the kids had to rely on the masking tape trail. Suddenly, Jenny stopped short and whirled around to face the boys.

"OMG!" She grabbed both their arms. "What time is it?"

Matt pulled out his cell. "Ten-seventeen."

She squealed and clapped her hands. "That means that Gus Allen and Jay Wilcox will be here soon." She smoothed back her hair.

"And Nancy Mulligan," Matt added, grinning.

Jenny pursed her lips. "That's right. Maybe we can stop into town and you can buy her some flowers."

"You can buy some, too," Matt said. "You know it's okay nowadays for girls to give dudes flowers. I bet Gus and Jay would be all 'oooh, we got flowers from that twelve-year-old blonde girl.'"

"Um, guys," Steve said quietly.

"At least they'd acknowledge me," Jenny said. "From what I hear, you'll be lucky if Nancy Mulligan even looks at you."

"Guys!" Steve said.

"What?" Jenny said. "We're just messing with each other."

"We've lost the trail." Steve bent down and picked something out of a nearby bush. "Or, should I say, someone wants us to lose the trail." He held out his hand for the other two to see.

"Is that our masking tape?" Jenny took the object from his hand.

Steve nodded. "Someone took it off the tree, wadded it into a ball, and threw it into this bush."

Jenny searched the ground around them. "But I don't see any footprints but ours. Are you sure someone did that? Maybe it was an animal."

Matt gulped. "Or a ghost."

"No animal out here would have the ability to tear the masking tape and wad it into a ball." Steve sighed and added, "And ghosts wouldn't be able to physically grab the tape."

"So, you think someone *wants* us to get lost?" Jenny said.

Matt looked around. "Not to freak anyone out or anything, but I think it worked. I have no idea where we are."

"Spread out," Steve ordered. "Perhaps we can find more masking tape and pick up our trail."

As the trio split up, Steve did not feel at all confident about finding any more tape. If someone wanted them to be lost, they would have destroyed all the tape from here to the movie set. Steve frowned. But how could they have done it without leaving footprints?

After several minutes of searching, the kids regrouped, all having found nothing.

"What now?" Jenny asked, a twinge of nervousness in her voice.

Steve pulled the compass from his pocket and opened it. The needle pointed north, left from their current location. He gave a short miserable laugh. "Well, this might have been more useful if I had used it when we started. I have no idea what direction we traveled to get here."

Matt's eyes widened. "Hold up. *I* know."

Jenny narrowed her eyes. "Are you being serious, because this is not a time for jokes."

"No, I'm being totally serious," Matt said. "Remember when we left the set? The sun was on our right, and now, check it out." He waved his hand up to the sky. "It's higher, but it's still not directly above us because it's not noon yet. That means that east is in that direction." He pointed. "So, to get home..."

"...we need to travel south." Steve finished and nodded. "Good thinking, Matt."

"And good memory," Jenny added. "I wasn't even paying attention to the sun."

Matt shrugged. "It's from all those years of camping."

Steve glanced at his compass. "I guess we really didn't need this with Matt around." He started to put it back in his pocket, but Matt stopped him.

"No, dude, leave it out. We're gonna need it when that sun gets a little higher in the sky. Once the sun is directly over us, we won't be able to tell what direction we're going."

Steve nodded and the kids began their trek south.

"I hope we're not super far," Jenny said. "I'm so thirsty."

"Me, too," Matt said. "We really should've brought more water with us."

After sipping the last of his own water, Steve agreed. "We must plan better next time."

Suddenly, the ground started to shake.

Steve looked around wildly.

"Earthquake!" Matt yelled. "Get down!"

11 THE ROSIEST ROSE

Steve held his breath as the tremor lasted only a few seconds then stopped.

"Not a very big one," Jenny commented as she got up and resumed walking.

"Yeah," Matt agreed. "I hope it didn't cause any damage to the set."

As he watched a few loose rocks slide down the nearest hill, Steve felt his heart racing inside his chest. He shook his head. "I don't think I'll ever get accustomed to those."

Matt nodded. "I keep forgetting that you didn't grow up in Cali like we did."

"We've been used to them since we were in pre-school," Jenny said.

"Hey, Jenn." Matt wiped some dust off his shirt. "Remember that time in first grade when we all had to climb under our desks?"

Jenny chuckled. "And Mrs. Abbott got mad at you for going into your desk to grab your lunch box first."

"Hey, I had a cold-cuts sandwich and a couple bags of Cheetos in there. I wasn't about to let the earthquake take them."

Grabbing Matt's arm, Jenny wiped some more dust off his sleeve. "Remember how all that stuff fell off Mrs. Abbott's walls?"

"Oh, yeah," Matt said. "She made us all go around and pick everything up. Isn't that like free child labor or something?"

Steve stopped walking, an idea forming in his head.

Jenny looked at Steve, her eyebrows knit together. "Steve, are you okay?"

"That's it!" Steve said. "That's what we're missing!"

Matt frowned. "We're missing free child labor?"

"No," Steve said, wondering why he hadn't thought of it before. "The flower stones. That's the reason they were scattered and some were upside-down."

Matt shook his head. "Dude, you lost me."

"Me, too," Jenny added. "What are you talking about?"

"The stones weren't all scattered originally," Steve explained. "When Josiah Carney carved them, they were all on the side of a cliff. But, at some point, between when he died and now, an earthquake must have shaken the stones loose."

"I get it," Jenny said. "Big earthquakes always cause rocks to come loose and fall off the mountains."

"Okay," Matt said, "if that is what happened, then how do we find where the original etched rocks were?"

Steve bit his lip. "The rocks we found all seemed to be in one general area, if we scout around, I'll bet we find the mountainside they came from."

"Can we come back and do that?" Matt asked as he looked up at the sky. "The sun's getting intense."

Steve hesitated. "I know we're all thirsty and that we really should go back for water, but the film crew will be returning soon," he paused.

"And," Jenny continued, "if we try to come back later, we might not be coming back alone."

Noticing the doubtful expression on Matt's face, Steve continued. "And the sooner we finish this, the sooner we can go back and eat lunch. I heard they're having a taco truck and—"

Matt raised his hand to get Steve to stop talking. "Dude, you had me at lunch."

Steve grinned. The three detectives reversed direction and headed back toward the etched stones.

Upon reaching the location, they split up, this time searching the nearby cliffs for any sign of the carved stones.

After a few minutes, Jenny called out, "Hey, guys, over here."

The two boys joined her, and she pointed to the cliff in front of her. "Look," she said, excitement in her voice. "I think I found it!"

Steve examined the cliffside. Dirt and small rocks covered most of the face, but several faint etchings of flowers were visible through the dirt. He spat on his thumb and rubbed one of the etchings. A distinct flower came into view. "This is it all right."

"So now what?" Matt asked.

"Let's see what Josiah tells us." Steve scrolled through his pictures until he found the poem. *"Then you can walk away and go to the land of flowers. Choose the rosiest and smell it hard. Then the real work begins."*

Matt scratched his head. "I think I've asked this before, but how can you tell which flower is the rosiest?"

Steve scrunched his forehead in thought. If the flowers had color, then it would be fairly easy. The kids would just need to find the reddest rose. But the flowers were all etched into stones. Tan stones. None of them would be rosy at all. He shook his head. "It has to be a metaphor for something."

"Like what?" Jenny asked. "I mean, if you

asked me what girl in school had the rosiest cheeks, I'd tell you Melanie Sampson because her cheeks are like always red. I don't see any of these rocks having rosy anything."

Matt put his hand to his chest. "A rose by any other name," he paused and then mumbled, "something, something, something."

Jenny rolled her eyes. "Seriously, Matt, if you're going to try and quote Shakespeare, you should at least get it right."

"Well," Matt said, "how does it go then?"

Throwing her arms up in dramatic fashion, Jenny inhaled a deep breath and said, "*A rose by any other name would smell as sweet.* It's something Juliet said when she was talking about Romeo's last name."

"Hm," Matt said. "Think that would work on Nancy Mulligan?" He placed both hands over his heart. "Nancy, you are like a rose, and smell as sweet as…as…, wait, how did that go again?"

Jenny laughed. "Maybe you should stick to tacos, Romeo. Don't you think so, Steve?"

No response.

"Steve?" Jenny repeated and looked back.

Still no response.

Matt shook his head. "Looks like we lost him again."

"That's it," Steve said suddenly. "Matt, you're brilliant!"

"I am?" Matt said.

"He is?" Jenny said.

Both sounded surprised.

Steve chuckled. "What I mean is that the Shakespeare line you quoted is the secret to the riddle."

"How so?" Jenny asked.

"All the flowers you saw on the rocks we picked up earlier," Steve said, "how many of them were roses?"

Jenny teetered her head back and forth as though thinking. "None of them, actually."

"Matt?" Steve asked.

Matt shrugged. "I don't know. I wasn't really paying attention, but I remember that most of them looked like those Easter flowers. I don't know what they're called, but my mom gets them every year and puts them in our living room."

"Lilies," Jenny said.

"That's it!" Matt snapped his fingers. "Lilies. Most of the flowers I saw on the rocks were lilies."

"Exactly," Steve said. "So none of those would be the *rosiest*. We need to find the etching of a rose. Let's split up."

"But what if the rose was one of the rocks that fell off during the earthquake?" Jenny asked.

"That is a possibility," Steve admitted. "But let's start by examining the cliff wall. Perhaps we'll get lucky."

The trio split up, each taking a different section of the cliff.

Steve moved to the far left and studied every flower intently. Some were so covered in dirt that he had to wipe them with the sleeve of his shirt. After fifteen minutes, Matt came up and joined him.

"Any luck?" he asked

Steve shook his head. "You?"

"Nope."

Jenny walked up to them. "You guys find anything?"

Steve shook his head. "Unfortunately, no. But the rose has to be here someplace."

"Maybe it's one of the flowers that fell off," Jenny suggested.

Steve sighed. "If that's the case, then it may be harder than we thought to find the rose."

"Hey, guys," Matt said. "Check this out." He picked up a rock from the ground. "Doesn't this kinda look like part of a rose?"

Snatching the rock from his hand, Jenny held it up close to her face. "Believe it or not, I think Matt's right. Look." She handed the stone to Steve.

Steve studied the rock carefully. The etching of a flower did resemble a rose, but the flower was not complete. "It looks like the stone broke when it came off the cliff." He began surveying the floor. "The rest of it is probably around here someplace."

The kids got on their hands and knees and

began picking up all the rocks in the area. After a few minutes, Steve sat on his knees and rubbed the sweat from his forehead. Something on the cliff wall caught his attention. He stood and walked over to examine it. "Guys," he said, excited by his find. "It's over here."

Jenny looked up from the ground. "Where?"

"The other part of the flower," Steve said. "It's still attached to the wall."

As the other kids gathered around him, Steve held up his broken piece of the rose to the etching on the wall to complete the flower. "A perfect match."

"Great!" Matt said. "Now what?"

Jenny pulled out her phone while Steve kept the broken stone in its place. "According to the miner's note," she said, "we're supposed to *Choose the rosiest and smell it hard. Then the real work begins.*"

"What does that mean?" Matt frowned. "We're supposed to smell a rock?"

"And not just smell it," Jenny said. "Smell it hard."

Steve studied the flower. Most it was still attached to the wall, only about a third of the rose had come loose and fallen off. "Perhaps he meant for us to push the flower into the wall."

"You think that's what he meant by smell it hard?" Jenny asked.

"I don't know," Steve admitted. "Let's try it. I'll keep the broken piece in place while one of you pushes the flower."

"I'll do it," Jenny said.

Steve placed his right fingers on the very top of the flower and his left fingers over the bottom and then moved to give Jenny room.

Jenny put her right hand on the entire flower and pushed. "Ugh," she said, but nothing happened.

"You may need to push a bit harder," Steve said.

"Matt." Jenny moved to the side. "You're the strong one. You try it."

Jenny and Matt switched places and he positioned his right hand on top of the flower with his left on top of it. "Here goes nothing." He pushed as hard as he could, but nothing happened. After several tries, he stepped back, wiping his forehead with his arm "It's not budging."

"Maybe it's been too long," Jenny said.

"Or, maybe it's broken," Matt suggested. "We do get a lot of earthquakes in this area. What if it broke during a big quake?"

Steve did not respond. What they were saying made sense, but he had a feeling that was not the case. "The poem must mean something else."

"Like what?" Matt asked. "Steve, dude, I know you want to find this treasure and all, but the temp is rising pretty fast and we've got no more water.

We need to go before we turn into little piles of dust and vultures try to pick at our bones."

Jenny sighed. "Sorry, Steve, but I'm with Matt on this one. We can't be out in this sun for too much longer. One or more of us is gonna get sick and then we're really stuck."

Steve knew they were right. He could already feel his tongue and the roof of his mouth dry from the heat. He licked his lips. "Okay, let's try one more thing and then I promise we'll get out of here."

"Okay," Matt agreed. "One more thing. What did you have in mind?"

Steve hesitated. "Smell the flower."

"What?" Matt frowned. "You mean like smell the rock?"

"Perhaps the instructions are literal," Steve said, "and we have to smell the rose."

Matt heaved a heavy sigh. "All right, stand back. Let's get this craziness over with so we can get back to civilization and a giant soda." He put his nose up to the rock, and after one last glance at Steve who nodded, he took a whiff and began coughing. "Dude, it's dusty."

Steve wiped the flower, both the intact part on the wall as well as the small broken piece, as best he could. "There. That should be better."

"And remember," Jenny said, "you've got to smell it hard, so take a good, deep sniff."

Matt tossed his head back. "Ugh. The things I do for this team."

"And that's why we love you," Jenny said and gave him a quick hug.

Looking from Steve to Jenny, Matt narrowed his eyes. "I hate you guys."

Jenny and Steve laughed.

"Love you, Matt," Jenny said.

Matt shook his head, then exhaled all the air from his lungs. He put his nose right up to the flower, closed his eyes, and inhaled deeply.

12 A DANGEROUS PATH

Steve held his breath, waiting.

Moments later, Matt was coughing and rubbing his nose. The worst part, nothing happened.

Jenny reached into the side pocket of her backpack and pulled out a tissue. "Here. I brought this in case my allergies kicked in, but I think you need this more than I do. Blow your nose and try to get all that dust out."

Feeling bad, Steve was about to apologize to his friend, and then it hit him. "That's it!"

"What's it?" Jenny asked as she watched Matt blow his nose several times into the tissue.

Steve didn't answer. Instead, he placed the broken flower piece on the ground and examined the flower portion on the cliff. He ran his fingers around it until he found what he was looking for, a groove encircling the flower. With a little maneuvering, he cleared the groove of dirt. "I think this piece of the wall comes out."

"What do you mean?" Jenny asked.

Steve turned to his friends, his excitement mounting. "Remember on our first mystery, when we were inside the first cave? We found the burning bush and then removed the wall behind it."

"You think that's what's going on here?" Matt asked, sounding completely stuffed up.

Steve cringed a little, feeling bad for not figuring it out before Matt got a nose full of dirt. "I think when he said to smell it hard, he didn't mean to literally smell it, but rather to pull it toward you as though you were inhaling it."

"Now you tell me," Matt mumbled.

"Sorry," Steve said meekly. "If it makes you feel any better, it was Jenny telling you to blow your nose hard that gave me the idea."

As he stared at Steve through narrowed eyes, Matt blew his nose again.

Steve turned to face the rock. "I traced a groove around the flower. I'm going to try and pull it out." He slid his fingertips into the groove and tried to pry the rock loose. "Oof," he said, accomplishing nothing.

"Let me try." Jenny gave him a slight push. "My fingers are smaller than yours." She shifted her fingers around and then pulled. The rock moved a few centimeters. "It's working!" She tugged again, and the rock budged a few centimeters more. She paused to catch her breath. "This might take a while."

Once she had moved it a couple inches, Matt took over and pulled the rock out completely. He set the basketball-sized fragment on the floor. "Now what?"

Steve peered into the newly uncovered hole on the cliff side. "There's something in here." He reached his hand inside and felt around. "It feels like a fat ring attached to a lever."

"Well," Jenny said, excitement in her voice, "what are you waiting for? Pull it!"

Hooking his index finger inside the ring, Steve gave a strong pull. The lever moved easily enough, about three inches, before it stopped and clicked.

The three friends stared at the opening.

"Was something supposed to happen?" Matt asked.

Steve frowned. "I don't—" The ground started to shake beneath them.

"It's another earthquake!" Jenny said.

"Come on!" Matt grabbed Steve and Jenny's arms. "We need to get away from the cliff!"

The three friends staggered away, and within seconds, the shaking stopped. Behind them, a cloud of dust floated up toward the sky.

Steve studied the surrounding area. "That's odd."

As she wiped dust off her shirt, Jenny asked, "What's odd?"

"The only area affected by the earthquake was the cliff. Look around. There are no other dust clouds. It's as if the earthquake hit only—"

All three friends looked at each other and smiled. It hadn't been an earthquake, it was a secret compartment opening up.

As they walked back to the cliff, Matt commented, "You know, this is feeling more and more like our first case."

"Right?" Jenny laughed. "I'm waiting for Mr. Alexander to pop out any minute now and threaten us to find the treasure for him." She was referring to the international jewel thief whom, in their first case, had threatened the kids to find the Magic Sapphire or he would hurt two of their schoolmates.

"Don't joke about that," Matt said. "He got out of jail, remember?"

"Yeah, "Jenny said, "but if he were out here, I'm pretty sure we would've seen him by now."

They reached the place where the flower etching had been and stared at the cliff wall.

"Seriously?" was all Matt could say.

"Are we supposed to go through that?" Jenny said.

The lever had indeed created an opening in the cliff wall, but the hole stood only about eighteen inches round.

Steve scrunched his forehead in thought. "Remember what Alysha said about the miner's friend, Allen Jacobs? He was a small guy wanted in a bunch of states for burglary."

"That's right." Jenny nodded. "He was so small he could get away through tiny places where the police couldn't follow him."

Squatting, Matt peered into the opening. "I get it. Elias made the hole big enough for his friend to get through but too small for most adults."

Steve grinned. "But not too small for three twelve-year-old kids."

"Hold on," Matt said. "How do we know there aren't booby traps in there? Remember Elias Darby? The man put crazy traps everywhere."

"Yes," Steve acknowledged, "but, in that case, the pirate was trying to keep people away from the treasure. In this case, the miner *wanted* his friend to find it."

Seeing the nervous expressions on both his friends' faces, Steve pulled out his cell phone. "Let's see what our next instructions are. *Choose the rosiest and smell it hard. Then the real work begins. Squeeze like a lemon and then roll like dough.*"

"Well," Matt commented, "I think we know what he meant by squeeze like a lemon."

"What do you suppose the next part means?" Jenny asked. "The *roll like dough* part?"

"Let's focus on one part at a time," Steve said. "Ready to squeeze like a lemon?"

"I don't suppose there's any chance that there'll be a nice, cold lemonade at the end of this, right?" Matt said.

Steve grinned. "Not likely."

Matt sighed dramatically. "All right. Let's get this craziness over with." He got on hands and knees and crawled to the opening. He paused before entering. "You sure there're no traps?"

"Absolutely," Steve said with certainty in his voice. "No traps."

Matt laid his body flat on the ground, then, crawling army style, he slowly disappeared into the hole.

"How's it going?" Jenny said loudly. She sounded nervous.

"Ugh." Matt's voice came out of the hole. "It's tight, but at least there aren't arrows flying over my head. Hey, I think I see a break up ahead. Hold on."

Steve waited patiently for Matt to speak again. Within seconds, he heard him, although he sounded a little muffled.

"I'm through. It's not too bad, just keep your butt down or you'll scrape it on the ceiling."

"I'm coming next." Jenny laid herself down on the ground. As she disappeared into the tunnel, Steve thought about the poem. Could it really be that no one, not even Jacobs, had figured this out?

He thought about Sam and Peggy and wondered how far they had gotten.

"I'm through." Jenny's voice interrupted his thoughts.

Steve got down on his stomach and began the crawl into the tunnel. The dirt scraped his arms a bit, but the thought of another earthquake hitting while he was in there caused him to hurry. Less than a minute later, he stood on the other side next to his friends.

As he studied their new surroundings, Steve tried to evaluate the situation. They were in a cave, maybe twenty feet round, with holes scattered throughout, allowing sunlight in. The shade of the cave's ceiling felt good after hours under the morning sun. "At least it's cooler in here," he commented.

"That's for sure," Matt said. "What's next?"

"Here's the rest of the note," Steve said. "*Squeeze like a lemon and then roll like dough. If you make it through the giant pipe and find my box, you're almost there. All you need is a shovel.*"

"Okay." Jenny looked around. "So, now we're supposed to roll like dough. Whatever that means."

"Scatter and examine every part of this cave," Steve said. "Somewhere lies the key to getting out of here and finding that treasure."

They split up, each studying a different part of the cave walls. Steve wasn't sure exactly how rolling like dough would get them out of here, but he knew there had to be a hidden way out and they needed to find it.

"Hey, guys," Jenny said. "Over here." As the boys crowded around her, she pointed to a small etching on the wall at almost eye level to them. "It's a drawing."

"Is that..." Matt paused and squinted at the mark on the wall, "...a loaf of French bread?"

Steve nodded. "It would appear that we have found our *dough*."

"And it's making me hungry," Matt added.

After running her fingers over the etching, Jenny turned to Steve and frowned. "How exactly are we supposed to roll like it?"

Steve scratched his chin. "Well, Carney would have created a way for Jacobs to exit the room, so let's see if the French loaf can provide us a way out." He leaned in and tried pushing in the picture to see if that would open a hidden passage. Nothing happened.

"Maybe it's like the last picture," Matt suggested, "and we have to pull it out."

Steve tried to find an outline around the bread like he did the rose. Nothing. He scowled. "I don't get it. There has to be a hidden way out of here."

"Try it again," Matt said.

Steve obeyed, shoving with all his might. Nothing.

"Dude," Matt said, "I think I saw something. Do it again."

With renewed enthusiasm, Steve pushed harder.

"Down here." Matt squatted and pointed to the ground. "When you push the French bread, the ground moves. Watch. Do it again."

While Steve did as instructed, he fixed his eyes on the ground. Just as Matt said, when Steve pushed in the picture, the ground below the picture shifted.

"Do you think it's another tunnel?" Jenny asked.

"Yes." Steve kneeled and began pulling dirt away from the wall. "But, I believe the reason we didn't see it at first is because all this dirt is in the way. Help me clear it out so we can get to the tunnel."

The three kids began digging the dirt away from the wall beneath the picture. After a few minutes, they hit rock.

"That should do it." Steve stood, determined to figure out the last clues and find the treasure. He placed his hand on the picture again and pushed it in.

This time, a segment of the ground, two feet across, lowered at an angle, like a slide. It remained open for ten seconds then returned to its normal position.

"What do you think?" Matt asked.

"I think we need to roll like dough," Steve answered and got down on the ground.

"Hold up, Steve," Matt said. "Maybe I should go first.

"I'll be okay." He crawled to the opening. "Okay, open it up."

Jenny pushed the picture but nothing happened. She tried again. "Ugh. I think it's stuck."

"Here," Matt said and motioned for her to move to the side. "Let me try." Matt shoved the picture hard and the ground lowered. "Looks like you've got to push it really hard."

Steve lowered his feet inside like one would do when going down a slide. "Here goes nothing." He shoved himself forward before the ground closed on him. Soon, he was sliding down a dirt path at full speed. He hit a bump. "Ow!" Unfortunately, the bump caused his body to turn slightly and soon he was tumbling down, out of control. He hit the bottom, hard, and groaned. That would leave a few bruises for sure.

He stood and yelled up. "I'm down. Be careful!" No response. Steve figured he was too far down for his friends to hear him. Unlike the cave he had just been in, this place was pitch black. He pulled out his cell from his pocket hoping he didn't damage it in the fall.

He pressed the button and the screen came to life. Relieved he wouldn't have to explain a broken

143

cell to his parents, he turned on the flashlight and then heard movement and squealing coming toward him. Jenny landed at his feet.

"Are you okay?" he asked, offering his hand to help her stand.

She took his hand and shakily stood. "That was like the worst thing ever. My whole body hurts."

A few seconds later, Matt came tumbling down and groaned as he hit the bottom. "Never let me do that again."

Jenny and Steve helped him up, and then the three kids dusted themselves off.

"Well," Matt said and turned on his flashlight app. "Where are we now?"

"I don't know." Steve shone his light around. "I haven't had time to look."

Matt pointed to the right. "It looks like a tunnel over there."

"That might be the only exit," Jenny said as she scanned around. "I don't see any other way out of here." She rubbed her arms. "It's chilly down here."

"We did fall for quite a while," Steve said. "And do you notice the smell?"

"You mean the smell of wet dirt?" Matt said. "Yeah, kinda hard to miss."

"Why would it be wet down here?" Jenny asked.

Steve shrugged. "There's probably an underground water supply around here somewhere."

"Dude, do you think it's safe down here?" Matt said, suddenly sounding uneasy. "I mean, if this place floods, we're goners. There's no way we'd be able to climb back up that hill. Come to think of it," he paused, "we're totally stuck down here. We can't go back the way we came."

"Then we must find a way out," Steve said, trying to sound more confident than he felt. He had already thought of the fact that they had no back-up plan for getting out. If the tunnel turned out to be a dead end, or blocked by earthquake rubble, they had no way of escaping. They would be trapped down there, forever.

13 THE MINER

Steve still stood in silence, contemplating their safety, when Jenny spoke.

"Okay," she said, sounding as nervous as Matt had a moment ago, "so is this tunnel the only way out of here?"

After contemplating her words, Steve hit his head with the palm of his hand. "Of course, the tunnel is the way out. Remember the last part of the miner's note? *If you make it through the giant pipe and find my box, you're almost there.*"

Matt shuffled his feet. "I'm not sure I'm liking the word *if* in that sentence. It makes it sound like we may not make it out."

"I know what you mean," Jenny said. "But, we don't exactly have a choice."

Matt shone his light into the tunnel. "Dark, never-ending tunnel of doom, here we come."

The trio moved slowly inside, scanning the walls for anything dangerous. As they moved, Steve noticed the temperature dropping and his shoes sloshing. They were now trekking through mud. No one said anything.

After a few minutes, Steve saw what he suspected to be a dim light ahead of them and stopped.

"What's going on?" Jenny asked in a voice barely above a whisper.

"There's a light up ahead," Steve replied in an equally low voice.

"Do you think we're there?" Jenny asked.

"Wherever *there* may be," Matt mumbled.

Steve said nothing and resumed leading the group toward the light. Soon, they reached the end of the tunnel and found themselves inside a large cavern about the size of a convenience store.

Steve shone his light around the cavern and froze. Two people sat on the ground not twenty feet away from them.

"Is someone there?" a timid female voice spoke out.

Steve recognized the voice at once and shone his light in her direction. "Peggy?"

"Who's there?" She sounded frightened.

Slowly, he walked toward her with his friends right behind him. "It's me, Steve, from the movie set."

As he got closer, he noticed that she sat with her back to the wall, a rope tied around her body. She blinked at the bright light from his phone.

He knelt beside her. "Peggy, what happened?"

"How did you kids get down here?" She asked, then shook her head. "Never mind that, you have got to get out of here. Hurry, before he comes back!"

"Who?" Steve asked. "Sam?"

Peggy's eyebrows shot up. "You know about Sam?" She shook her head. "No, it's not Sam. It's…it's…the miner."

"Whoa," Matt said. "Did you just say, the miner?"

Peggy looked terrified. "I know it sounds crazy, but we saw him. He's the one who dragged us down here."

A moan reminded Steve that someone else was there, laying on the ground a few feet away from Peggy. He shone the light on the man and saw that he was semi-unconscious.

Jenny tugged lightly on Steve's sleeve and pointed. "Is that…Grant?"

"Listen," Peggy said, "you kids have got to get out of here. The miner, he's crazy."

"I don't understand," Steve said as he knelt to examine the rope tied around her. "How could it be the miner?" He reached for his pocketknife and began slicing through the rope.

"I…I don't know," Peggy stammered, "but he's real."

Grant, fully conscious now, struggled to sit up, but he, too, was tied with rope. "Oh, my head. What happened?" Steve watched him as his eyes landed on the kids. "What are you kids doing here?"

Matt gave a short laugh. "Would you believe we're looking for the treasure?" He pulled out his pocketknife and began to cut Grant's ropes.

"I wish I had never even heard about this stupid treasure," Grant muttered.

"Where are Sam and his accomplice?" Steve asked.

Peggy looked hesitant, then finally said, "They split not long after we found the body of their friend, Kevin, and I wanted to call the police."

Matt gulped. "What do you mean you found *the body*?"

"It's a long story," Peggy began. "Kevin went missing a week ago. We thought he had just given up on the treasure hunt, but then, a couple days ago, we found his body. He had been stabbed. Grant and I wanted to call the police, but Sam threatened us, saying if we called the cops that he'd take care of us."

"I get the feeling Sam is wanted by the cops," Grant said.

"He is." Steve finished cutting Peggy's ropes. "For arson and armed robbery."

"How do you know that?" Grant asked.

"It was part of our investigation," Steve answered.

"Investigation?" Grant repeated. "As in, detectives?"

"The Decoders, to be exact," Jenny said, sounding very proud.

The rope fell off Grant and he rubbed his arms. "Hold on, the Decoders? You were the ones who helped at the Coppertown set?"

Matt grinned. "Yep, that was us."

Steve put his knife away. "Jack called to tell us about the treasure, and then invited us to the set. He had no idea Sam or you were actually looking for it."

"How did you guys hook up with that Sam dude, anyway?" Matt asked. "You don't seem like the type to hang around mass criminals."

"We can swap stories later." Peggy stood. "Right now, we need to get out of here before the miner comes back."

"The miner," Steve repeated. "I still don't understand."

"I don't, either," Peggy said, "but he's real. And...crazy. We have to go."

"None of you is going anywhere," a grizzly voice sounded behind them.

Steve whirled around and stared in disbelief. It was the miner, exactly as the pictures depicted him, right down to the scraggly mountain-man beard. In his right hand, the man held a gun, the same handgun he held in the photograph at the museum.

"It…it can't be," Steve stammered.

The miner chuckled. "That's what everyone be sayin', but here I am. Now, sit down, the lot of ya." He shuffled toward a large barrel on the side of the cavern, taking the smallest of steps, like those that a toddler would make.

Steve bit his lip as he sat on the ground. This was impossible, he couldn't be real. That would make him nearly two hundred years old. Steve eyed the man carefully. He had to be someone in disguise. A very elaborate and well-crafted disguise. Everything was perfect, down to the last detail.

The miner pulled a bag out of the barrel and then fumbled with something inside it while keeping the gun steadily aimed at the kids. Soon, he left the bag and hobbled in front of the group.

"What is it you want?" Steve asked.

The miner looked at him with a curious expression. "Same as you, I reckin. My treasure."

Steve kept a steady gaze on the man. "If you really are Josiah Carney, how is it you don't know where the treasure is?"

The man let out a mild curse. "Cuz that fool of a friend of mine moved it. I took all that time to write out the directions, and he up and moved the treasure, the dang fool."

Never taking his eyes off the man, Steve asked, "Why would he do that? Why not just take the treasure with him?"

The miner gave an evil grin. "Cuz you can't take it with you when you go." He pointed up to the ceiling.

"You mean," Jenny said, "Jacobs is dead?"

"Long time now," the miner said. "1851."

Steve frowned. "But, that's the same year you died, allegedly."

"That's right," the miner said. "Bumbling fool came after the treasure and didn't bring no water, no provisions."

"Sounds familiar," Matt mumbled.

"Found his body right outside the cave here, I did." Josiah scratched his chin. "Problem is, he'd already moved the treasure, don't nobody know where."

"Why would he do that?" Steve asked.

"Cuz he didn't want me to take it back once he'd found out I was still alive."

Matt cleared his throat. "Not to be rude or anything, but, dude, how *are* you still alive?"

"Yeah," Jenny added. "The coroner declared you dead. Like *dead* dead."

The miner chuckled. "Was I now?"

Steve felt his eyelids getting heavy. He blinked several times, trying to stay awake. To his side, he saw Jenny and Matt both collapse on the ground.

Peggy and Grant fell next. Steve fought the tiredness, but realized the truth as his body crashed to the ground. They had all been drugged.

14 ESCAPE!

Steve tried to remain awake, but his eyelids slowly closed on him. Through the corner of his eye, he saw the miner stand up straight, and then everything went black.

Steve gradually came back to consciousness. After blinking several times, he felt his head reeling in pain. He tried to move his hands, but couldn't.

"You okay?" The question came from Peggy. "Steve?"

He looked around and saw Peggy and Grant tied up with rope in the same manner as when the three kids first found them in the cavern. Matt and Jenny were also tied up, but lying on the ground. He tried to get up then noticed that he, too, was bound with rope.

"What happened?" he managed to say.

"We were drugged," Grant said, sounding a little annoyed, "again."

"Is this what happened to you last time?" Steve asked.

Grant nodded. "We were digging around in here when the miner showed up. He pulled out his gun, which I thought was a fake, until he shot off a couple rounds into the ceiling."

"He talked to us for a little while," Peggy added, "just like he did with you guys, then we both got dizzy and woke up like this."

Matt groaned. "Oh, my head." He sat up and struggled with the ropes for a moment.

Jenny turned over. "What happened?"

"I think we were hit by a truck," Matt said. "At least, that's what it feels like."

Peggy and Grant explained to the two kids what they had already said to Steve.

Matt frowned. "So, this miner dude drugged us?"

"It would appear so," Steve said.

"Why?" Matt asked.

Steve tightened his lips. "Good question." He turned to Grant. "You mentioned that you and Peggy were digging in here. Were you looking for the treasure?"

Grant nodded. "Yeah, we've been coming here at night, when we're both free, and digging around the cavern. Since we had such a long break after the sunrise shoot, we thought we'd get in some extra time."

"Wait," Matt said, a look of confusion on his face. "How did you get in here? I mean, no offense, dudes, but that first hidden tunnel was small as anything. *I* barely fit in there."

"Are you saying you kids figured out the miner's note?" Peggy said.

"Yes," Steve answered. "We followed each of the steps laid out by the miner." He paused. "How did *you* get here?"

Grant laughed. "By total luck. We were snooping around the area, mostly just for kicks, then Peggy stumbled down a hole—"

"—and almost broke my arm." Peggy interjected.

"Right," Grant said. "I told her to hold tight and went back to get some rope. Then, I tied the rope to a tree and lowered myself in here. We used our flashlights and found the miner's box."

"But we had a shoot coming up," Peggy continued the story, "so we came back later and brought a ladder." She motioned with her head to a ladder leading to a small hole in the ceiling.

"You found the box?" Steve said, completely engrossed in the story. "What was in it?"

"Wait, wait, wait," Matt interrupted. "Are you saying we scoured the desert dying of thirst looking for flower rocks, got dirt shoved up my nose (some

157

of which is still there, by the way), army-crawled through the smallest tunnel on the planet, and then slid down the rockiest, bumpiest hill, got bruised black and blue, and all this time we could've used…a ladder?"

Peggy flashed him an apologetic smile. "Sorry about that."

"Come on, Matt," Jenny said, grinning. "Think of it as character building. And, believe me, you definitely need some of that."

Matt threw her an evil look. "I hate you."

"So, what was in the box?" Steve asked again. "Were there additional instructions?"

"Or, some of the treasure?" Jenny said.

"No." Peggy shook her head. "That's just it. The box was empty. Although," she paused for a moment, "it did have one word inscribed underneath: *Laquear.*"

Matt frowned. "Isn't that the name of a paint finish?"

"Yep," Peggy said, "although it's spelled a little different. It's also the name of a furniture company, who I would guess made the box."

"So, basically, the box had no clue for us," Grant said. "But we figured since the box was *here*, in this cavern, and that was the last instruction on the note, this is where the treasure had to be buried."

"Apparently," Peggy said, "so does the miner.

Many of the holes around here must be his, because we didn't make them."

"Which brings me back to this miner," Steve said. "Any idea who he is?"

"Dude, isn't it obvious?" Matt said. "It's Josiah."

Steve shook his head. "It is *not* Josiah Carney."

"You're right." Matt nodded. "It's his ghost."

"It is not Josiah's ghost or any other ghost for that matter," Steve said, wishing his friend would let the whole ghost thing go. "The miner is a real, live human being, dressed up to look like Josiah."

"Why would anyone go through all that trouble?" Jenny asked. "I mean, the guy looks and acts just like him, right down to the short steps."

"I don't know," Steve admitted. "Perhaps he doesn't want anyone to identify him. Which means," Steve paused as he realized the truth, "he's someone on the set. Someone we'd all recognize."

"What?" Peggy and Grant said simultaneously.

"Actually," Jenny said, "that makes sense. Who else would have access to the wardrobe and make-up needed to pull this off?"

Steve nodded. "It's also why we've never seen any evidence of him around—no campsite, no garbage."

"No way, dude," Matt said. "You mean we've been eating dinner next to the miner without even knowing it?"

"I can't believe it's someone we know," Peggy said, shaking her head.

"What I don't get," Grant said, "is why kill Kevin?"

"Perhaps Kevin figured out who he was, Steve said, "and the miner decided to silence him before he told anyone."

Matt gulped. "So, if the miner has no problem silencing people, then what's he gonna do with us?"

"Good question," Grant said. "Why hasn't he killed us yet?"

Steve scrunched his forehead in thought. They were still missing something, something important. He could feel it. "Peggy, how many people were with you the night you guys knocked us unconscious?"

Peggy stared at him blankly. "What?"

"You know," Matt added, "the night you all clobbered us then left us out for wolf food."

Grant's eyes widened. "Wait. What happened now?"

Steve could tell by the expressions on both Peggy and Grant's faces that they had no idea what the kids were talking about. "You weren't there," he said slowly as an idea began to form in his head.

Between Matt and Jenny, the two of them related to the adults what had happened that night. Steve was only halfway listening, his mind trying to piece everything together.

Steve suddenly turned to Peggy. "When did you meet Sam?" The question probably seemed to come from out of the blue, but it was imperative for him to get a timeline.

Peggy arched her eyebrows, apparently surprised by the question. "Um, sometime near the beginning of the shoot. Grant and I were out looking for the treasure, more for fun than anything else. We ran into Sam, John, and Kevin out here and we just kind of formed a partnership."

"We agreed to split the treasure five ways when we found it," Grant added.

"And there was no one else?" Steve asked. "Besides the five of you?"

Both Peggy and Grant shook their heads.

Steve set his jaw. "There is another person. Someone with Sam and John the night we were attacked."

"Wouldn't that be Kevin?" Jenny asked.

Steve shook his head. "That doesn't fit with the timeline. According to what Peggy said and what we overheard, Kevin disappeared long before we were attacked."

"That's right, he was stabbed," Jenny said and shivered. "What happened to his body, anyway? Is it still out there?"

"Sam and John buried it." Peggy sighed. "We should've just called the police."

"Hold up," Matt said. "If Kevin wasn't the

third guy out there the night we were attacked, then who was?"

"My money's on the miner," Jenny said.

Steve shook his head. "Think about how we got out of there."

"Okay," Matt said. "Some dude with a gun scared away the wolves."

"Wait!" Jenny said. "Steve, you think the miner is the guy who saved us?"

Steve nodded. "It makes sense. This miner hasn't actually hurt any of us."

"Uh," Matt interrupted, "massive headache from being drugged. That counts as hurting."

"My point is," Steve said, "he could easily have killed us all if he wanted to. There's nobody out here. No witnesses. And nobody even knows where this cavern is, so he could easily get away with it."

Jenny frowned. "So, what's his deal, then?"

Unsure if his theory made sense, Steve hesitated. "I think the miner is trying to keep us safe."

"Safe from what?" Matt said.

Steve tried not to sound ominous with his answer, but couldn't. "The killer."

"You mean the man who killed Kevin?" Grant said.

"And, I believe, Sam and John," Steve added.

"Wait," Peggy said. "Sam and John aren't dead, they just split after they buried Kevin."

Steve looked at her. "You know him better than I, but did Sam seem the type to run out on a treasure because a friend of his was killed?"

"No," Grant said, "Sam was the type to find whoever did it and make him pay."

"OMG," Jenny said. "You think that Sam and John are dead and were killed by the same guy who killed Kevin?"

"Yes," Steve said solemnly. "And I think the miner knows who it is."

"Wait," Grant said, "if the miner is someone from the set, then the killer probably is, too."

Everyone was silent for a moment.

"We need to get out of here," Grant said.

Steve nodded. "I agree."

Matt struggled with his ropes. "I'm open to ideas."

Laying down, Steve felt the knife still in his pocket. The miner had not removed it. He jiggled around hoping to get it to slide up and out of his pocket, so he could grab it with his hands.

"Uh, you okay, Steve?" Matt asked.

Steve chuckled realizing how ridiculous he must've looked. "I'm good. Just working on a plan." A couple more jiggles and the knife slid out. "Got it!"

"Got what?" Jenny said, throwing him an odd look. "A case of the jitters?"

He grinned. "My pocketknife. Matt, move over

here with your back to mine so I can cut the ropes off you."

"You're brilliant, dude." Matt scooted across the ground to Steve.

Once Steve felt Matt's ropes in his hands, he began cutting, careful not to accidently cut flesh by mistake.

After several minutes, the ropes dropped off Matt, who jumped up, shouting, "I'm free! I'm free! Take that, miner dude."

"Great," Jenny said. "Now untie the rest of us, you dolt."

Matt pulled out his own knife and the two boys released the others from their restraints.

"Hey, everyone." Grant pointed to one of the side walls, "there's a case of water over there. The miner must've brought it down here."

Jenny clapped her hands. "OMG, I'm so thirsty I could drink a whole river."

"Thank you, miner dude!" Matt jumped over and grabbed a bottle. "I say we take the water and split."

"I second that," Steve said.

Jenny agreed. "Best plan I've ever heard!"

Matt unscrewed the lid to his water. "Really?"

"No," Jenny said as she reached for a bottle. "I just wanted to make you feel good."

Matt sighed dramatically. "Thanks a lot."

Everyone laughed and chugged their water.

Within seconds, empty water bottles dotted the floor of the cavern.

"I feel kinda bad leaving them here," Jenny said. "It's not exactly environmentally friendly."

"They would be more of a burden to take with us," Steve pointed out. "When this is all over, we can come back and dispose of them properly."

The group gathered around the ladder.

"I'll go up first," Grant said, "and make sure the coast is clear. If so, I'll call down and you all can climb up."

As Steve watched Grant climb up the rungs, he thought how odd it was to have an adult leading the way. The only adult that had ever really helped them with their mysteries was Tyrone, and even he rarely went on the missions with them. He was more like their informant, as well as the best chef in Beachdale.

Grant disappeared and then a few seconds later announced, "It's safe!"

Jenny went up next, followed by Peggy, then Steve, and Matt came up last.

Steve blinked and looked around. The sun sat much lower than when they began. He hadn't even given a thought to the time. He glanced at his phone. 4:30. "It's getting late."

Grant looked at the time on his cell and cursed. "We're supposed to be on set in half an hour. Jack's going to flip when we're not there."

"He's gonna flip a lot more when he finds out there's a killer on set," Matt said.

"What do we do now?" Jenny asked.

"We go back and tell Jack to call the police," Steve said. "Until the killer is found, we need to stay close to the set, and away from the desert."

"Smartest thing I've heard you say," Matt said, grinning. "I'm all about staying safe."

"But, Steve," Jenny said, "if the killer is one of the people on the set, are we really safe there?"

Matt gulped. "I take it back. Not the smartest thing you've said."

Steve shook his head. "Whoever the killer is, he's never struck on site. In fact, the only people he's killed are people who've gone after the treasure."

"Like us," Matt grumbled.

"That's why we need to get back to the set ASAP," Steve said, suddenly realizing their urgency. "As long as we're out here, we're in danger. Grant, you know how to get back to the movie set from here, right?"

"Yeah, follow me." He moved toward a dense collection of bushes and climbed through them. A few scratches later, the group found themselves on a path.

"That cavern entrance is totally hidden from here," Matt commented. "How in the world did you guys end up there?"

Peggy pointed back. "We were following this path, and then, just where those bushes are, I saw a group of red foxes. They were beautiful and the camera woman in me took over. I climbed through the bushes trying to get a good angle to take their picture, and that's when I fell through the hole."

"That was some pretty crazy luck," Jenny said.

Peggy shook her head. "Yeah, and all bad. Now three people are dead and all of us are in danger. I wish I had never stumbled on that stupid hole."

"Steve," Matt said, "you've been pretty quiet since we left the cavern. Everything okay?"

"I've been trying to figure out the identity of both the miner and the killer," he answered.

"Any luck?" Jenny said.

"Not really." He sighed. "I saw the miner when we were filming from the balcony of the hotel, remember?"

"That's right," Jenny said. "You said you saw him one minute and then he was gone."

"Correct," Steve said. "And, when we went out to examine the spot, we saw his footprints, and then they also disappeared."

"You know what all this means, don't you?" Matt said.

"Don't...say...it," Steve warned.

"Please," Jenny begged.

"What?" Grant asked. "What does it mean?"

Matt looked solemn. "The miner is a ghost."

Grant chuckled.

"You had to ask," Steve groaned.

"Hey," Matt protested. "It makes sense. The dude just up and disappears. What other reason could there be?"

"About a hundred other logical ones," Steve said.

Matt crossed his arms. "Well, I haven't heard you say one yet."

"Matt," Jenny scolded, "He's not a ghost! We saw him. We spoke to him. He tied us up."

Matt raised a finger in the air. "Aha! Did we see him tie us up? No, we did not. We were all in nighty-night land."

"And you think, what?" Jenny frowned. "He used his supernatural powers to magically place the ropes around us?"

"Maybe."

Jenny rolled her eyes. "Ugh. I am *so* done talking to you."

"Perhaps we can focus on something a little more…earthly," Steve said. "Like where the miner got his attire. Peggy, the clothes the miner was wearing, did it look like they came from the set's wardrobe trailer?"

"To be honest, I don't know," Peggy admitted. "It's possible. We have so many different costumes, it's hard to keep track. But, Lydia might know, or at least she'd know if one was missing."

"That gun was definitely no prop," Grant said. "That was the real deal. And not a hokey imitation, either. It's authentic."

Steve scrunched his forehead. "Who would have access to an authentic old-time handgun?"

"A collector, maybe," Grant said. "Those things would be hard to come by, I can tell you that. My dad's a collector. He'd give his left eye for one of those."

"Are there any collectors on the set?" Steve asked.

Grant shrugged. "Not that I know of, but that doesn't mean there aren't."

"Steve," Jenny said, "not to change the subject, but how are the police going to catch the killer?"

"What do you mean?" Matt asked. "The same way they always do."

"That's what I mean," Jenny said. "There aren't any dead bodies. The killer disposed of them. No one has seen the killer, so we can't even, like, give the cops a description."

"And I intend to keep it that way." The chilling voice came from behind them.

Steve whirled around and froze. He could not believe his eyes. "You!"

15 A DEADLY FOE

Of all the people Steve thought could be the killer, this was not one of them.

The old man smiled an evil grin while pointing a very large gun at the group. "Surprise."

How could Steve have been so wrong? The killer wasn't a person from the set at all. It was the one person who knew more about the miner than anyone else in the world. Suddenly, it all made sense.

"Hold up." Matt held up his hands in a stop movement. "*You're* the bad guy?"

The museum docent teetered his head back and forth. "If that's the way you want to put it."

"You killed three people," Steve said solemnly. "I think *bad guy* may not be a strong enough description."

The man waved his free hand around. "Bah.

It's not like the three of them were angels or anything. I did society a favor killing off those three. Now, you all, that may be a different story."

"Wh...what do you mean?" Matt stammered.

"He means that killing us may be a little more complicated." Steve said.

"Oh, good," Matt said. "As long as he knows that."

"Complicated, yes." The docent took a few steps closer. "But certainly not impossible."

"We're due on set any minute now," Grant said. "When we don't show up, they'll start searching for us."

The docent laughed. "Haven't you heard? The shoot's been canceled. It seems the flight carrying your big celebrity stars from Los Angeles got delayed. They're not coming in until tomorrow, so Jack gave everyone the night off. Looks like no one's going to be missing you for a while. And, by the time they find your bodies out here, the wolves will have taken care of any evidence, and that's assuming they even think to look out this far from the set."

Steve realized he needed to keep the docent talking until he could figure out a plan. "I don't understand. You've been the museum docent for years. Why do all of this now? Why kill three men?"

The man snarled. "Those amateurs thought they

were going to take my treasure. If anyone deserves that gold, it's me."

"Why is that?" Steve asked, as he glanced around. There had to be something they could use as a weapon. But he saw nothing.

"I've run that museum for forty years, and every day off, every holiday, I've been out here searching for that treasure. That gold is rightfully mine, just like it was my great-great-grandfather's."

Steve frowned. "You're related to Josiah Carney?"

"Not Carney," he said and shook his head, "Jacobs. That note rightfully belonged to my ancestor, Allen Jacobs. People thought the note was a fake, but I know better. Because I found this."

With his free hand, the docent pulled out a folded piece of paper from his pocket. "It's a copy, I've got the original locked up. But this letter predates that one in the museum. It's from Carney to my great-great-grandfather, begging him to take care of his daughter Elizabeth, if anything happened to him. And, if it did, he would leave instructions and sufficient resources for his daughter to be well taken care of."

As the man returned the paper to his pocket, Steve took advantage of the distraction to reach into his own pocket and slightly lift out his cell. In seconds, he pressed the emergency call button and released the phone back into his pocket. It was a long shot considering cell service didn't quite make it out there, but a long shot was better than nothing.

"So, you see," the docent continued, "the treasure is real, and it belongs to me."

"There's still something I don't understand," Steve said trying to delay as long as possible. "If all this is true, then why didn't your great-great-grandfather come to retrieve the treasure?"

The docent's eyes narrowed. "Because he never received the note Carney left to be delivered upon his death."

"The one in the museum?" Steve said.

The man nodded. "Once it became known that Carney had hidden that gold and that his last note was the clue of how to find it, the note didn't get delivered. Instead, the townspeople decided to put it on display for the whole world to see, to drive people to come here and spend money. It revitalized the town, at least for a little while." His eyes flashed in anger. "Imagine, those townspeople denying my family what was rightfully theirs, all to make some money for themselves."

Steve tried to keep the man talking. "Technically, the treasure belongs to Carney's descendants. He left that money for your ancestor to take care of his granddaughter. If that gold rightfully belongs to anyone, it would be her descendants."

"There aren't any of her descendants left." The

elderly man's face broke into a wicked grin. "At least, not anymore."

"Wh...what does that mean?" Matt asked.

Steve thought about it for a moment. The pieces slowly came together. "Kevin was her descendant, wasn't he?"

"That's right," the docent said.

Steve thought back to the small paper the kids had found in the prop shed. "The paper, the one with the numbers. Those were latitude and longitude coordinates. It belonged to Kevin, didn't it?"

The docent applauded. "You're pretty smart for a kid. But what you don't know, is how Sam got a hold of that paper. He and his buddy held up a bank and took everything from the safe deposit boxes, including an old diary left behind by Carney's granddaughter, talking about the gold and the mysterious note with the numbers her grandfather had sent her a few weeks before he died. Sam figured out the story, tracked down Kevin, her one descendent, and then came here to find the gold. The fool stopped by the museum to learn all he could about Carney and showed me the diary and the paper, hoping I could tell him what the numbers meant. I knew right away it was latitude and longitude, so I made a copy and then came out here to search for the gold myself."

"That's why you killed Kevin," Steve said. "As

Carney's descendant, the treasure rightfully belonged to him."

"I thought Kevin's disappearance would scare Sam off," the elderly man paused and pointed the gun at Grant and Peggy, "but then these two helped him figure out what the numbers meant, so Sam decided to stay."

"So, you joined up with them, too," Steve said, trying to work it all out. "It was you with them that night we were attacked. You drugged Jenny."

He nodded. "Sam wanted to knock you all off right then and there, but I convinced him that leaving your bodies for the wolves would be more believable to those who found you. Bullet holes would be conspicuous, and cops would swarm the place."

"Why turn on Sam?" Steve asked.

"He and his buddy started talking about how they were going to spend their part of the treasure, and how we would still be rich after splitting it five ways. Five ways! Those crazy fools. I knew I had to take care of them."

"And that's why you killed them," Steve said.

"It was either them or me, and Sam was already wanted by the police for murder. I knew nobody would be missing those two, and I wasn't about to let them split the gold." He pointed to Grant and Peggy. "I would've killed these two as well, but I couldn't find them. Until now, that is."

"And, after all this," Steve said, "you still haven't found the treasure, have you?"

The docent frowned. "No."

"Maybe someone already found it," Jenny said. "Like, years ago."

The elderly man shook his head. "I would've known about it. A find like that couldn't be kept quiet. No, the gold is still out here. And I intend to find it."

Matt held up his hand. "Um, I have a question."

The docent eyed him carefully.

Matt continued, "What happened to Josiah's body? I mean, if the miner really isn't a ghost, then what happened to the dead dude's body?"

"Nobody knows." The man chuckled. "It's one of the great mysteries of our time."

Out of the corner of his eye, Steve thought he saw Grant eyeing the gun. If he was right, the stuntman was going to try and overtake the docent. Steve needed to help him. "Well," he said in a loud voice and tossed his hands up in dramatic fashion, "that's just great!" He swung his arms around. "We're all stuck out here, in the middle of nowhere, and all for nothing!"

"Uh, Steve," Matt said, a twinge of nervousness in his voice, "calm down, dude. Man with a gun, remember?"

The docent kept his eyes focused on Steve.

Steve laughed. "Yeah, that's the best part of all

of this, isn't it? We're all going to die, and for what? There is no treasure."

"Stop saying that," the man said, clearly becoming annoyed.

"Stop saying what?" Steve said, his voice escalating. "That your whole life was just a big, giant waste of time?"

"That's it." The docent turned his gun toward Steve's head. "You're dead."

With a burst of speed, Grant tackled the man and the two of them wrestled on the ground for control of the gun. Suddenly, a shot rang through the air and Grant clutched at his leg.

The docent scrambled up, gun in his hand, and aimed it at Grant. "Now you die."

"Freeze!" Someone shouted, and in a whirlwind of movement, ten fully-armed SWAT officers, guns raised, encircled the group.

The miner appeared and stepped through the circle of cops, only this time, his steps were not tiny and he held a modern handgun in his hands, aimed at the elderly man. "Drop the gun." The docent looked dazed as the miner walked up to him. "I said, drop the gun."

The elderly docent let his weapon fall to the ground and a nearby officer grabbed him from behind and placed him in handcuffs. "Christopher Bernshaw," the officer said, "you are under arrest for the murders of Sam Ellis, Kevin Wharton, and

John Drew. You have the right to remain silent…"
They disappeared into the shrubs, the policeman
reciting the docent his rights.

The miner bent down and examined Grant's
leg. "It doesn't look too bad. The bullet just grazed
you." He grinned. "You've had worse accidents on
set." He motioned to a nearby EMT to come over.

Squinting, Grant pointed at the grizzled old
man. "No way. You're the miner?"

The man grinned widely and took off his wig,
fake beard, and then peeled off a face mask.

"Brian?" Steve, Matt, and Jenny said
simultaneously.

"W-ell," he said and teetered his head back and
forth, "sort of."

"OMG!" Jenny's eyes widened. "I can't believe
you're the miner."

"I know, dude," Matt added. "You sure had me
fooled."

"That was kinda the plan," Brian said and stood
to give the EMT more room. "Come on. Let's leave
the medic to do his thing and head back to the
movie set, get you guys some food, and then I'll
explain everything afterward."

"Dude." Matt smiled. "You had me at food."

On the way back, Steve thought about all that
had just happened. Brian being the miner started to
make sense. He would've easily been able to track
Grant and Peggy's outings because he and Grant

were roommates, and he would have no problem going in and out of the wardrobe trailer.

The docent being the killer also made sense. He had access to all the knowledge of Josiah Carney, including direct contact with the note.

The only thing that still bothered Steve was the treasure itself. Even with the latitude and longitude coordinates, and the location of Carney's box, no one had been able to find the treasure. The possibility existed that the gold was a hoax, but Steve didn't think so. Somehow, a piece to this puzzle was missing, and until he figured it out, they wouldn't be able to find the gold.

Once they reached the set, Brian went to explain things to Jack, Grant was taken to the medical tent to have the on-site doctor finish treating his wound, and the three kids, after a quick stop to change their very dirty clothes, went to the mess tent where the smell of Mexican food dominated the air.

Matt inhaled deeply as they went to get plates. "Oh, man, I love Mexican food."

"Not to restate the obvious," Jenny said as she grabbed some silverware, "but you love all food."

He grinned as he reached the beginning of the buffet. "I know, but Mexican's got to be one of my all-time favorites."

Nodding, Jenny scooped some guacamole onto her plate. "Yeah, me, too."

Steve only half-listened to the conversation, his mind focused on the treasure. What were they missing?

Once they heaped their plates, they headed toward an empty table and sat down.

"This may be one of the craziest days we've ever had," Matt said as he plowed his fork into a mass of rice and beans. "I'm starving."

"I totally agree with you," Jenny said. "On both counts, the crazy day thing and the starving thing. We haven't eaten anything since like six o'clock this morning."

Matt gulped down his enormous mouthful of food. "And my belly knows it. Don't worry." He patted his stomach. "I'll take real good care of you right now."

"Mind if I join you?" Grant asked as he approached the table.

"For sure, dude," Matt said. "Grab a seat."

Steve noticed the man limping. "How are you doing?"

"Okay," he said. "Brian was right, the bullet only grazed me. Doc patched me up and gave me some pain pills. What I really need is some sustenance."

Matt took a swig of his soda. "I recommend the chimichanga. It's amazing."

"The enchiladas are super good, too." Jenny added.

"And the fajitas. And the tamales." Matt added.

Grant laughed. "Guess I'll get a little of everything. Brian said he'd be over here soon to explain things. Don't let him start without me."

"Will do," Jenny said.

After a few minutes, Grant returned with a plate piled almost as high as Matt's. He winced as he moved his leg to get it over the bench seat. "That's gonna hurt for a while."

"Thanks for trying to save us," Jenny said. "That was, like, really brave."

"Totally, dude," Matt said. "You're the man."

"I don't know about that," Grant said. "Steve's the one who distracted the guy with his crazy ramblings. Once the guy turned his gun to Steve, I knew that was my one shot."

Jenny put down her fork and looked at Steve. "So, that's why you went all crazy like that?"

"Dude," Matt said. "I thought for sure the heat had gotten to you and you were seriously freaking out."

Steve grinned. "All part of the plan."

Brian walked up. "Mind if I join you? I'm guessing you have a few questions."

Matt moved his plate over to make room for Brian. "You have no idea."

"Perhaps you should start from the beginning," Steve said as the man sat down. "Who exactly are you?"

He inhaled a deep breath. "My real name, coincidently, *is* Brian, but Brian Iverson, not Metcalf. I work for the F.B.I., assigned to track down and bring in Sam Ellis for armed robbery and murder. We knew that Sam was operating out here, but we didn't know what he looked like, because he always wore masks during the robberies, and his name, Sam Ellis, was an alias. We're still waiting on fingerprint analysis to determine his real name.

"I posed as Brian Metcalf to get myself onto the set. The real Brian Metcalf is actually recovering from an injury, so we asked permission to impersonate him to catch Sam. No one on the set, not even Jack, knew my real identity."

"For an impersonator, you did some impressive stunt work," Grant commented.

Brian laughed. "To tell you the truth, it was pretty fun. And, believe it or not, way safer than my usual assignments."

"What was with the miner thing?" Matt asked. "I mean, nobody knew your real identity anyway, so why dress like the miner?"

Brian shifted in his seat. "The problem was that I couldn't exactly be snooping around as Brian Metcalf, either. Once I figured out the only reason Sam would be here was to look for the treasure, I started scoping out the surrounding area. If people saw me roaming around the desert, they'd start asking questions, so I decided to come up with a disguise. The rumor of the miner seemed like the best option, so I did a little research and put together the outfit."

"What about the gun?" Steve asked. "From what Grant said, that model is pretty rare."

He took it out from his holster. "Yeah, I borrowed this from a friend up in San Francisco. I had to promise him my left arm if I damaged it." He flicked it around. "It's pretty cool, though, right?"

They all agreed.

After placing the gun back in his holster, he continued. "I knew Sam had at least one partner, but, again, I didn't know who it was. I figured my best shot at finding them was to try and track them at night in the desert. I didn't even know about Kevin's death until I heard you all talking about it in the cavern."

"How did you learn about the cavern?" Grant asked.

"From you and Peggy," he said. "I followed you one day, thinking maybe you'd lead me to Sam. That was the day Peggy fell into the hole. After that, I came back to the cavern a few times hoping to catch Sam, but somehow, we always managed to miss each other."

"I saw you once," Steve said, "the afternoon we shot the balcony scene. We tried tracking you, but couldn't find you. Then we found your footprints, but they disappeared."

"That's right," Jenny said. "Actually, we had that problem a few times, the footprints mysteriously disappearing."

Brian nodded. "I had that same problem tracking Sam. I finally figured out that the whole area is overrun with dust devils. They just come up out of nowhere and dissolve just as fast"

Steve mentally scolded himself for not deducing that himself. "We should have figured out that's what happened to the footprints."

Grant turned to Brian. "When did you figure out something more than just treasure hunting was going on?"

Brian continued. "One day I heard you and Peggy talking about calling the police but being afraid to because of what Sam might do. I almost revealed myself then, but decided against it, just in case Sam decided to use you against me.

"Once I found the bodies of Sam and John in the desert, I called in for reinforcements, but they couldn't get here until later today. That's when I knew I had to get you guys out of the killer's way."

Grant frowned. "So, you knocked us out and tied us up?"

"I know." Brian winced. "But it was for your own good. I intended to track the killer, get him in custody, and then come back and release you and Peggy. But I couldn't find him. So I came back to untie you and found a new set of prints. The killer was close by. But then, you and the kids showed up out of the blue and I knew I had to keep you all safe until my help arrived."

"How did you drug us?" Steve asked. "I didn't see you spray anything into the air."

"It's an F.B.I thing," Brian explained. "I kept the drug canister in my duffle bag, and then opened the can when I needed to drug you all."

Steve frowned. "But why didn't the drug affect you?"

"Because I spent a lot of time building up an immunity to it."

"Um," Matt raised his hand. "I have a question."

Brian grinned. "Okay, shoot."

"Did you find the treasure?"

"No," Brian said and shook his head, "can't say that I did. But, to be fair, treasure hunting wasn't exactly my mission here."

Jenny sighed. "But it was ours. And we failed."

"Not yet we didn't," Steve said as a smile spread across his face.

Matt arched an eyebrow. "What do you mean?"

"I mean, we never found the treasure because we were interrupted. If we go back to the cave, the one where Grant and Peggy found the miner's box, we still have a chance to find it."

"I'm in!" Jenny said.

Steve turned to the two men. "What do you

guys say? Are you up for one more shot at a treasure hunt?"

Brian teetered his head back and forth. "I've got quite a bit of paperwork to get through tonight, but I think I can squeeze in some time for treasure hunting in the morning."

"Wish I could," Grant said wistfully. "This leg's got me laid up for a while. But," he paused and pointed to the kids, "I think if anyone can find that gold, it'll be the three of you."

Brian stood. "I've got to stop in and see Jack anyway, I'll let him know the plan. I'm sure he'll be okay with it, especially since his main actors have been delayed until tomorrow, anyway."

A thought struck Steve. "Was that you? Were you the reason their flight was delayed?"

Brian grinned. "Yeah, Gus Allen knows the real Brian Metcalf. I couldn't let him see me or he'd know I was a fake."

After Brian left, the three kids talked with Grant a while longer, then finished their dinner and headed back toward their trailers.

Matt stretched his arms over his head. "Man, I'm so tired, I could sleep for a hundred years."

"Make that like two hundred years." Jenny yawned.

As Steve lay in his bed, he thought about the miner, the real miner. The man had left coordinates and a coded message, so clearly, he wanted his friend, and *only* his friend, to find the gold, but then why leave a box with no clue?

On a hunch, Steve reached for his phone. He did a search for lacquer and got several definitions as well as the furniture company Peggy mentioned. Steve scrunched his forehead in thought. Peggy also mentioned that the spelling was a little different, perhaps that was significant.

After several searches, Steve found what he was looking for. Smiling, he put down his phone and relaxed into bed. Tomorrow, the Decoders would solve this mystery once and for all. He knew the location of the treasure.

16 THE MINER'S "GOLD"

The next morning, after a hearty breakfast, the three detectives and Brian headed into the desert and toward the cave. Steve had not told his friends about his discovery the night before; he wanted to wait until he saw the box for himself to be sure.

"Just so you all know," Matt said as they approached the entrance, "when we find the gold, I'm going to open a Mexican restaurant in Beachdale."

"I don't think that's a good idea," Jenny said.

Matt frowned. "Why not?"

"Because," she said with a twinkle in her eye, "you'd eat all your profits."

Matt opened his mouth as if to respond, then laughed. "Yeah, you're probably right."

"I hate to put a damper on your treasure hunt," Brian said, "but I had my guys back in DC do some digging. It turns out the miner's family still owns a stake on this property."

"The docent said there were no descendants alive," Steve said.

Brian shook his head. "He was wrong. There are six living heirs to the Carney fortune should we actually find it."

"Aw, MAN!" Matt sounded disappointed. "I was really looking forward to owning my own restaurant."

"Cheer up, Matt" Jenny said. "At least, this way, you'll still be able to fit through the door of your house."

After climbing through the dense bushes, Brian knelt at the cavern entrance and put his flashlight in his pocket. "Be careful climbing down." He lowered his legs into the hole until his feet were planted firmly on the steps and then began his descent into the cave.

Jenny went next, followed by Steve and then Matt. Once at the bottom, each of them turned on the powerful flashlights that Jack had lent them.

"Where's the box?" Steve asked.

Brian pointed to the far side of the cave. "Grant said he and Peggy left it pretty much in the same place they found it."

The group walked over and saw the box sitting on the ground. Steve picked it up, opened it to reveal its empty contents, and then flipped it upside down to read the inscription. He smiled. It was just as he suspected.

Matt looked over his shoulder. "Well, that's not much help."

"Actually, it is." Steve handed him the box.

"Really?" Matt said, turning the box around with his hands. "Because I don't see anything but the inscription of that paint name."

"And that's all we need to see," Steve said.

Jenny clapped her hands once and pointed to Steve. "You figured out the clue."

Steve grinned. "Yep. Last night, while I lay in bed."

"Hold up." Matt stopped rotating the box. "You figured out where the treasure is, and you didn't tell us?"

Steve nodded slowly. "Sorry, but I had to see the box for myself to see if my theory was correct, and it was."

So," Jenny said, motioning with her hand for Steve to continue, "where is it?"

"The word laquear on the box," he said and pointed, "look at the spelling."

Matt shrugged. "What about it?"

"It's spelled wrong," Steve explained. "At least, wrong for the English word for the type of wood finish."

"You lost me," Jenny said.

Steve took a deep breath. "The word laquear, at

least, the way it's spelled here, isn't an English word. It's Latin."

"What does it mean in Latin?" Brian asked.

"Ceiling."

Watching his friends' expressions, Steve chuckled when every flashlight beam immediately turned upward.

"So, the treasure is in the ceiling?" Jenny asked.

"That is the only logical conclusion," Steve replied.

Brian nodded. "That would explain why neither Peggy and Grant nor the docent could find the treasure."

"But, how are *we* supposed to find it?" Matt asked. "I mean, if it's buried in the ceiling and all."

"The same way we discovered all the other clues," Steve answered. "We search for something either out of place or related to the miner."

The group split up, scanning their flashlights beams over different sections of the cave ceiling. Steve focused on the area directly over the location of the box. Soon, he spotted it. "Over here."

As the group gathered around him, he pointed to a spot above him. "See that?"

Jenny squinted. "Is that a picture of a rose?"

"Oh, no. Don't look at me." Matt waved both his hands in a no-way motion. "I am not smelling any more dirt again. Ever."

Steve laughed. "Relax, Matt. I don't think we have to smell anything. This rose is the miner's way of telling us where the treasure is."

Jenny shone her light around. "But, how are we supposed to get to it?"

"I could be wrong," Brian said and handed his flashlight to Steve, "but I think, if Matt gets on my shoulders, he'd be able to reach it."

Matt gave his flashlight to Jenny. "Let's do this."

"Be careful," she said.

After hoisting the boy onto his shoulders, Brian moved so that Matt was directly under the rose etching. Matt moved his hands around the rose. "There's a groove around the flower. Hold on."

The others waited patiently while Matt used his fingers to dig the dirt out of the circular outline. "Okay," he said finally, "I think this thing will come out. You guys should probably stand back in case things start to fall."

"What about you?" Jenny said, concern in her voice.

"I'll be okay."

Jenny and Steve took only a few steps back, not wanting to be far in case anything went wrong.

Matt tugged on the piece of ceiling until it came out in his hand.

"Well?" Jenny said.

Matt reached his hand into the new hole in the

ceiling. "I feel something." He paused for a moment. "I think it's some kind of ring attached to a lever."

"Like the last one," Steve said. "Hey, the ring!"

"What about it?" Matt said, suddenly sounding nervous. "Is it dangerous? Is it a booby trap?"

Steve laughed. "No. I just realized why Josiah put rings on all his levers."

"Why?" Jenny asked.

"Remember what Alysha said about Jacobs' left hand?"

After a pause, Jenny clapped. 'That's right! He had a hook for a left hand."

"Arrrgh," Matt said in a terrible pirate voice, "let's find us the treasure!" While everyone laughed, he held up his right index finger like a hook, then placed it inside the ring and yanked on the lever. Dirt began falling from the ceiling. He coughed and pulled again. More dirt fell. "Dudes, I think a piece of the ceiling is moving. Hold on." He tugged yet again, and a rectangular piece of the ceiling began to come down, like the hatchway of an attic.

He pulled it far enough down so that Steve and Jenny could grab it, then jumped off Brian's shoulders. Between the four of them, they lowered the ceiling segment as far as it could go, then a thick piece of metal slid down creating a ramp from the floor up into the ceiling.

Matt pushed down on the metal. "It should hold us if we go one at a time."

"I'll go first," Steve said and then held up a hand when he saw Matt preparing to protest. "I'm the lightest so I should test the waters, so to speak."

Matt consented but did not look happy about it. Steve took a step onto the metal ramp. It felt sturdy enough. He placed the flashlight in his pocket and then, using both his hands and feet, he scampered up. He took a quick look around and called for the others to join him.

Once all four were inside, Steve surveyed the area. It resembled an attic in every aspect of the word. The area was barely over five-feet-tall so the kids could stand upright, and several dirt-covered crates stood scattered around, with cobwebs sprinkled about.

"Think those crates hold the gold?" Matt asked.

"Only one way to find out." Steve walked to the closest one and grunted as he attempted to lift the lid. It was too heavy for him.

"Allow me," Brian said. After handing Steve his flashlight, he firmly grasped the lid and heaved.

Once the lid had been removed, the four of them peered inside.

Matt frowned. "Um, this isn't gold."

Steve shone his light around the trunk then reached his hand inside. "No, but at the time, this was worth the same as gold. It's silk."

"I wonder if the other trunks hold the same thing," Jenny said.

They spent the next half hour opening all the remaining trunks. Each was full of different items, including tapestries, clocks, and a variety of jewelry. There were several gold nuggets interspersed throughout the various trunks, but not to the extent they had expected. They decided to return to the movie set and let Brian contact the owners to inform them of the discovery.

"I don't get it," Matt said as they walked back. "I thought Carney said he had hidden a bunch of gold."

Steve bit his lip. "I have a theory."

"Spill," Jenny said.

"Carney died in the height of the gold rush. It is conceivable that he thought the price of gold would continue to go down if people continued finding large quantities of it."

Brian nodded. "I see where you're going with this."

Matt pointed between Steve and Brian. "Could one of you fill me in on it?"

"If the price of gold continued to drop," Steve explained, "then owning trunk-loads of it would end up being worthless."

"I get it," Jenny said. "So, he bought up other stuff, stuff that would still be valuable even if the price of gold went way down."

Steve nodded. "Exactly. Like silk and jewelry. Those things would continue to hold their value even if the price of gold collapsed."

"Well," Brian said, "gold or not, those items will still be worth a pretty penny. Some of those clocks, alone, will be considered valuable antiques. I'd say you just made six people incredibly happy."

Matt sighed dramatically. "Not as good as owning my own Mexican restaurant, but...I guess that's still mucho bueno." He grinned and everyone laughed.

Back at the set, the trio related all they had discovered to Jack while eating snacks at the mess tent.

"I knew you guys would find the treasure," Jack said. "I'm just sorry you got into so much danger. I feel terrible about that."

"Don't feel bad." Matt pointed to the chips in his hands. "The food alone made everything worth it."

Steve traced the rim of his soda can with his finger. "Jack." Steve hesitated. "You know we can't let people know about what we did."

"I know." He nodded. "Brian, Grant, and Peggy all swore they'd keep your secret. Brian said, when he speaks to the families, he's going to attribute the location of the treasure to a secret group of detectives known as the Decoders."

Steve grinned. "Perfect."

"Hey, guys." Grant hobbled over to their table and sat down. "I just wanted to say good job! You solved the secret of the miner's gold."

"Hey!" Jenny whipped out her phone. "That's a catchy title. Maybe Alysha can use it for her next newspaper article. These secret private investigators known as the Decoders are getting pretty famous, you know. Last time, we, I mean *they*, made it on page four of our local paper."

"Congratulations!" Grant clapped. "Oh, and speaking of famous, you guys ready to meet some celebrities?"

Jenny stopped typing and looked up, eyes wide. "OMG. They're here?" She put her phone in her pocket and used her fingers to comb through her hair. "How do I look?"

"Stupid as always." Matt chuckled and stuffed his mouth with chips.

Jenny made a face at him.

Grant laughed. "Well, Nancy Mulligan's here, too. You know, in case you're interested."

Matt choked on his chips and reached for his soda.

"Now who looks stupid?" Jenny said.

"Come on." Grant stood. "If we hurry, we can catch them before they hit make-up."

Jenny and Matt both jumped up, nearly knocking Grant to the ground. Laughing, the kids followed Grant toward the make-up trailer, but, as his friends babbled on about the celebrities, Steve couldn't help but think about what they had accomplished in the past few days. They had solved a century-old mystery, found a treasure that was about to make six people very wealthy, and helped put away a murderer. Steve smiled. That may not make them celebrities, but it was good enough for him.

BOOKS BY ALBA ARANGO

The Decoders Series

The Magic Sapphire

The Lady Ghost

The Sleepwalking Vampire

The Mysterious Music Box

The Statue of Anubis

The Miner's Gold

The JJ Bennett: Junior Spy Series

Problems in Prague

Jeopardy in Geneva

Bedlam in Berlin

Danger in Dublin

Last Stand in London

ABOUT THE AUTHOR

Alba Arango is the author of the Decoders series as well as the JJ Bennett: Junior Spy series. She lives in Las Vegas, Nevada, where she is a retired high school teacher turned full-time author. She loves coffee and chocolate (especially together…white chocolate mocha is the best!).

To learn more about Alba, visit her website at AlbaArango.com.

Instagram @AlbaArango.007

Twitter @AlbaArango007

Facebook: Alba Arango Author Page

Made in the USA
Las Vegas, NV
28 April 2022